Asher's Anthology:
My Six Favorites

Asher's Anthology:
My Six Favorites

The Magic Glass—Die For Love

Asher Drapkin

Order this book online at www.trafford.com
or email orders@trafford.com

Most Trafford titles are also available at major online book retailers.

Printed in the United States of America.

ISBN: 978-1-4269-7944-6 (sc)
ISBN: 978-1-4269-7945-3 (e)

Trafford rev. 09/17/2011

 www.trafford.com

North America & International
toll-free: 1 888 232 4444 (USA & Canada)
phone: 250 383 6864 ♦ fax: 812 355 4082

Die For Love

Guest: Martin come here there's someone you should meet.

Martin: (*Smiles and sighs*) Oh yes.

Guest: Martin this is Rosa. She –

Martin: Actually this is the third time we've been introduced. We get the feeling that we are being brought together for some special purpose.

(*All the guests within hearing giggle and smile*)

Martin: Because this is a wedding celebration does this mean we are now engaged?

(*More laughter – from the young lady guests*)

Martin: (*Turns to Rosa*) I hope you're not feeling as embarrassed as I am.

Rosa: I'm not so sure – perhaps we should move towards the terrace together then they might just leave us alone.

(*As they move off the band begins to play the Blue Danube waltz*)

Martin: Would you care to dance Rosa? I have the impression you like dancing.

Rosa: You *are* perceptive Martin. Tell me how do you come to be invited?

Martin: The Grooms family and mine were neighbours for many years in Stuttgart. When the Nazis began increasing their power and influence we thought we'd make a new start here in Bad Harzburgh. And you – where are you from?

Rosa: I was born in a village in the Memel district of Lithuania. The Bride's family also come from Memel.

Martin: I see so where are you living now?

Rosa: My mother and I lodge with her sister my aunt Freda in Hamlin.

Martin: And your father?

Rosa: I'd rather not talk about him if you don't mind it's a long story

Martin: Oh I'm sorry to hear that – please forgive me for asking such personal questions after knowing you just a short time. The truth is Rosa I. . . I um feel deeply attracted to you. Oh dear I know it sounds foolish and –

Rosa: (Smiles) Why foolish? – do you think it's wrong to pay a lady a compliment after only a short acquaintance?

Martin: Well, perhaps – I usually take time to plan my course of action before I undertake anything.

Rosa: And my charm and beauty have bedazzled your senses? (Smiles provocatively).

Martin: I should have said that – are you making fun of me?

Rosa: No Martin – I think the reason why everyone is laughing is because the band has stopped playing and we are still dancing.

(They both laugh and Martin escorts Rosa off the dance floor and on to the terrace).

Martin: (Turns to face Rosa) Rosa I meant what I said I really do find you very appealing and –

Rosa: (Smiles and chuckles) Oh I see – now I'm only appealing – that is not quite as strong as attractive.

Martin: (Taken aback) No No that's not –

Rosa: Oh yes *yes* Martin – You said attractive when you were holding and touching me when we were dancing Martin – but now when we are just talking. . (Smiles provocatively) you find me just *appealing* I am disappointed.

Martin: (Steps forward and kisses her gently on the lips) Are you still disappointed?

Rosa: (In a non committal tone) that was a little appealing.

Martin: Then how about this (Kisses her passionately on the lips with a lingering kiss)

Rosa: (Whispers) *that* was attractive.

(For a few moments they just look at each other)

Martin: There is a nice cafe not far from here where they make the authentic Black Forest gateaux – would you care to join me?

Rosa: It sounds delightful – how could I possibly refuse? Mind you is it safe?

Martin: It's as safe as anywhere can be in these troubled times. Have you heard of (Lowers his voice to a soft whisper) the White Rose Society?

Rosa: Once or twice – is there really such a group?

Martin: The owner of the cafe and most of the patrons are. It is the one public place I can relax in.

Rosa: Is it far from here. These shoes are made for dancing not walking.

Martin: It's about ten minutes or so maybe quarter of an hour at the most. I could carry you part way if needs be.

Rosa: Any pretext to touch me. I'm surprised will all your charm you are not already married.

Martin: I'll explain everything whilst we have our coffee. Come on let's go.

(They go to their respective Cloakrooms,
gather their coats and make their way to the Cafe)

Rosa: So this is the place – I noticed it on the way coming. The Blue Angel.

Martin: Shall we sit inside. It'll be dark soon and the night air will feel chilly.

Rosa: I'll be guided by your local knowledge.

(They enter the main room which is half empty.
In one corner two men are playing chess)

Martin: Do you have any particular choice of table? Or are you going to change your mind at least three times like the other ladies I have known?

Rosa: I'd prefer the window table. Oh and by the way Martin *this* lady knows what she likes and who she wants.

Martin: And just where do I fit in among your desires.

Rosa: So far you are on track as a desirable but you should not be complacent.

Martin: In that case I'd better order the coffee and cakes. (He beckons to the waiter who slowly moves toward them). Would you like a menu or do you prefer to trust my judgement?

Rosa: I'm not sure perhaps –

Martin: The quality of my judgement is equal to the warm passion of my kisses.

Rosa: (With mock seriousness) In that case I'd better have a menu. (She smiles as Martin's face drops) Only joking Martin You order. Just remember what I said – you should not be complacent.

Martin: (Places order for coffee and cakes- then) Look Rosa I hope you will forgive me for being –

Rosa: Martin I've only known you for what – less than two hours and already you are going to propose.

Martin: (Looks blank) How on earth did you know that I ---

Rosa: I'm a woman Martin. Women always know. Don't look so bewildered.

Martin: Look Rosa I know – (The waiter returns with the order, and serves it up) Many thanks.

Waiter: Will that be all sir?

Martin: Yes for the moment thank you.

(The waiter gathers up the tray and leaves)

Martin: As I was saying mine gelippter sherne Rosa, Yes under normal circumstances in a different place, my proposal would sound and be absurd. (He lowers his voice and looks around the room) the way things are now war could break out at any moment and heaven alone only knows what is in store for us Jews. What I mean is there is no time for the courting game. Even though

I'm an engineer and used to detailed planning about everything I do – not just my work – but even in affairs of the heart: (He stretches out both hands and grips Rosa's hands) Please Rosa while there is still time I want to be your husband.

Rosa: (Smiling and in a tender tone says) Martin my love before I answer you there is something very important we need to do.

Martin: So tell me what is it?

Rosa: I think we should have a gateaux and drink our coffee before it gets too cold.

Martin: You really are incorrigible. Dare I say it is that what makes you so attractive and exciting? So what's your answer?

Rosa: Well let me see now. I've known you for about Two hours. We were introduced to each other three times by friends who must think that we are suited. You've already kissed me passionately. Bought me this delicious gateaux *and* coffee as well – How could I possibly refuse?

Martin: (Stands up, lunges forward and entwines his arms around Rosa's neck and kisses her) Rosa mine gelippeter sherne – I love you so – (At that moment the coffee table and all that's on it falls over as Martin kisses her again. The rest of the diners clap, cheer and shout 'Bravo Bravo.

Chess Player: I'm pleased you all appreciate my beautiful combination. A double pawn on the Queen's file and both my knights attacking the eighth rank.

(The other diners cheer even louder ironically –
Martin and Rosa join in)

Martin: There is a fancy Jewellers shop not far from here. I think we should pay him a visit.

Rosa: Sounds interesting – and just why would you like to take me there?

Martin: You'll see. On the way you can tell me all about yourself and I'll explain our wedding arrangements. Oh by the way did I mention that the ceremony will be tomorrow.

Rosa: Tomorrow? – I think –

Martin: (Takes her hand and leads the way out) I'll explain on the way.

Rosa: Martin – I know we have to rush but tomorrow!! I need to –

Martin: We have to act quickly –

Rosa: Yes I know that but even so how can you get a licence and find somewhere to have the wedding at such short notice? And besides I must inform my mother and –

Martin: Simple. We'll have a Jewish Ceremony without an official state licence. I'll have a word later with the Blue Angel Proprietor. That'll be the venue. All I need to know from you is how many guests will you bring?

Rosa: Just two – my mother and her sister. I suppose you've also worked out where we will live.

Martin: Sure – you'll stay in my apartment.

Rosa: Martin I've always dreamt of a whirlwind romance where a knight in shining armour would whisk me off on a white stallion to his private castle – but you've forgotten one thing.

Martin: Oh really – what's that?

Rosa: I'll need special permission from the state to change resident.

Martin: I'll sort it out me –

Rosa: You'll sort it out – how on earth can –

Martin: Mine dear gellipte sherne Rosa – for you I can do anything.

Rosa: Martin you say the sweetest things – but you're not a magician.

How can you possibly - ?

Martin: Simple – my younger brother is an officer in the Gestapo.

Rosa: (Taken aback) Martin please don't joke about –

Martin: (Laughs) I'm not joking – really. My father died when I was three years old and shortly afterwards my mother married a clock manufacturer – not Jewish. That is how I come to have a younger brother.

Rosa: That doesn't explain how he managed to –

Martin: Later Rosa later. This is the Jeweller's shop. After you.

(They enter the shop and the man behind the counter looks up. He is Martin's Uncle Gustav.)

Gustav: Martin – how good to see you – what brings you to my modest abode?

Martin: It's good to see you Uncle Gustav. My I present my bride to be – Rosa. Rosa this is my Uncle Gustav the kindest man in all Europe.

Gustav: (Kisses Rosa's hand) A pleasure to know you my dear. How long have you and my nephew known each other?

Martin: We were first introduced at 15.00 hrs this afternoon Uncle.

Gustav: (To Rosa) you may have noticed my dear young lady that my nephew is not only impetus – he is also precise. He couldn't simply say he met you this afternoon – he had to mention the exact time. Mind you I think you'll find all Engineers are Like that.

Rosa: I have noticed he makes decisions quickly.

Martin: When my Uncle and bride to be, decide to cease analysing my outstanding personality – perhaps we could look at some rings?

Gustav: (To Rosa) you may not have noticed just how modest my nephew is as well. Rings I'm afraid are in short supply but could I recommend these twin brooches. The red roses are very good quality rubies and the leaves are real diamond chippings.

Martin: I'll take them Uncle.

Gustav: I'm pleased *you* like them Martin – But perhaps your lovely bride might want to look at something else?

Rosa: They are very beautiful – I like them.

Martin: You see Uncle – I already have an instinct for Rosa's likes and dislikes.

Gustav: Very well. Where's the wedding and what time?

Martin: The Blue Angel tomorrow at three.

Gustav: I take it you have already made the arrangements

Martin: No not yet – I'll see to it after –

Gustav: No need Martin – the proprietor of the Blue Angel is an old friend. I'll see to it.

Martin: I'm in your debt Uncle – thank you very much.

Gustav: For you and your lovely bride nothing is too much trouble. Until tomorrow then.

(Martin and Rosa bid goodbye and continue on their way)

Rosa: Well Martin what other surprises do you have in store for me?

Martin: Well mine geliptte sherne let me see – oh yes the Rabbi who will conduct the service is from Poland. His brother who is a Sopher will be there as a witness and will write up the Ketuba. Also –

Rosa: Don't tell me – Herr Hitler will be the Best Man.

Martin: (In a mock serious vein) He's actually sent his apologies

He can't make it because he's busy making arrangements to invade Poland.

Rosa: Martin there's something you should know. I'm not in any way religious. I'm not really happy about having a religious marriage ceremony. I –

Martin: I'm not what you'd call Orthodox but I go to Synagogue on Yom Kippur. So far as the wedding goes – what alternative do we have? We've no civil rights now. Anyway why are you against our faith? Are you an atheist?

Rosa: I'm not sure. When I was a very young child – my father who was strictly observant in every way – suddenly disappeared. Then months later a stranger appeared at the front door. He handed my mother a document and calmly announced that my mother was now divorced. I still remember her tears. And I began to hate my father and all he stood for. I sorry if this seems wrong but that is what I feel and how I feel is who I am.

Martin: (After a longish pause) in some way I know what you mean. After my mother married someone who wasn't Jewish and no longer kept anything I too felt resentment. Although she still let me go to Hebrew school. My step father was an easy going man who wasn't interested in religion or politics – just work and sport. My Uncle who you just met is his elder brother.

Rosa: Your step-brother. What's *He* like.

Martin: Hans is a very charming man. Loves sport. He became a junior champion swimmer after I saved him from drowning when we were children. I taught him the basic strokes and from then on he never looked back.

Rosa: So how did he manage to join the Gestapo? With a Jewish mother the Nazis must have know he was Mishchelig.

Martin: To tell the truth I don't know for sure but I guess it's because his father invented and manufactured the Zimmerschaft Chronometer.

The family name is Zimmerschaft. My mother was always called Frau Zimmerschaft. So I suppose they assumed that he was one hundred percent Aryan – if you'll pardon the expression.

Rosa: I don't understand. Why should the son of the – what did you call it?

Martin: The Zimmerschaft Chronometer. Simple, my step father had the contract with the military and all the police departments to supply all the timepieces. Hans worked for his father as a Salesman and during the negotiations with the Gestapo they made him an offer of a Commission which he accepted. And – Oh here we are back at the –

Guest: There you are you two. Someone said they saw you slipping away. What have you been up to?

Martin: Nothing much – we went for a walk and a coffee at the Blue Angel and we decided to get married. Pass the word round. Everyone is invited to the Ceremony at the Blue Angel 15.00hrs.

Guest: Martin you are a joker – you know from your expression I almost believed you (Turns to Rosa) don't you think he's quite a comedian?

Rosa: He's not joking we are getting married tomorrow.

Guest: I *see* you are also a Comedienne –

Rosa: Yes I do have a sense of humour but we are getting married – honest. (Turns to face Martin) in fact I think I'd better introduce you to me mother and aunt. They're over there by the Bar.

Martin: (To guest as Rosa grabs his hand and pulls him away) don't forget – tell everyone tomorrow 15.00 at the Blue Angel.

(Fade out – then Fade in to Gestapo Headquarters Bad Harzburgh. The Oberst picks up his phone intercom)

Oberst: Zimmerschaft – in my office now.

Hans: On my way Herr Oberst.

(Hans gets up – knocks on door – waits)

Oberst: Komm.

Hans: You wanted me Herr Oberst.

Oberst: Yes come in, sit down – close the door. We have a problem lieutenant. In fact we have two problems. And they both concern you. The Sturmscharfuhrer of our Personnel Audit Division has found out that you gave false information when you joined the Gestapo.

Hans: With respect Herr Oberst – I answered truthfully all the questions put to me by the interview panel and furthermore I must point out that it was the Gestapo that approached me – I did not seek this post.

Oberst: I haven't finished lieutenant.

Hans: Sorry Sir – no disrespect intended.

Oberst: Quite – I am sure you are aware that your status is now classified as Mischlinge and as such you cannot remain in the Gestapo. Had you been honest with us at the beginning we might have been able to work something out. But now – you do understand.

Hans: Permission to speak Herr Oberst?

(The Oberst nods approval)

Hans: I'm sure sir my loyalty to the Fuhrer is confirmed by my excellent record. I am one hundred per cent a loyal German who works hard to see the fulfilment of the National Socialist dream.

Oberst: I'm glad you mentioned loyalty lieutenant, because you countermanded my deportation order regarding the Jew Martin Deutcher. Explain please.

Hans: I was not aware that you had raised a deportation order sir. My order to the staff was that Martin Deutcher must not be moved anywhere without my say so. And the reason is that Herr Deutcher is to undertake a special mission for the Luftwaffe.

Oberst: Explain

Hans: Generaloberst Von Shternbacher Luftwaffe Southern Command is a very close friend of my father's family. He has a serious problem the nature of which for security reasons I am not allowed to divulge.

Oberst: Lieutenant – I'm sure the Generaloberst is aware of procedures. He should have contacted the Head of Gestapo Bad Harzburgh and not a junior Lieutenant.

Hans: With respect Herr Oberst the Generaloberst was carrying out the orders of Reichamarschall Goering. It would not be appropriate to delay this mission for any reason.

Oberst: Lieutenant – It is not good for the morale of the Department when its Senior Officers are not considered to be trustworthy. I for one am deeply offended by this total disregard of discipline and protocol. It is further aggravating when a Mischlinge *is* regarded as trustworthy.

Hans: Perhaps Herr Oberst you would like to contact the Generaloberst about the matter? Or, if you prefer, I could contact him saying that you have countermanded my instructions?

Oberst: Are you threatening me Lieutenant?

Hans: Certainly not Herr Oberst. I am however placed in an invidious position. On the one hand I am under orders from a Generaloberst – on the other my status as a Mischlinge creates for me serious problems. What alternative do I have?

Oberst: And I am under orders Lieutenant to transport an exact quota of Jews per day. What alternative do *I* have? Have you any suggestions Lieutenant?

Hans: May I speak off the record Herr Oberst.

Oberst: Very well – off the record.

Hans: What I'm about to tell you is top secret and in absolute confidence. I am doing this because it is essential that we work closely together because we need each other. Agreed?

Oberst: Of course Lieutenant. Carry on.

Hans: In a matter of weeks or even days Germany will be at war. The outcome will –

Oberst: How can you be as sure as to the timing of the war?

Hans: The Luftwaffe has a few of its own Intelligence officers in Britain. They have close access to London's political circles. Not only is it known that the Fuhrer is planning to invade Poland very soon. This will force Britain to declare war. The Luftwaffe is concerned that our Messerschmitt will be up against an English fighter plane the Spitfire. So far there are rumours – or to be correct – strong rumours that the Spitfire can out perform the Messerschmitt. We need an agent inside the factory where the Spitfires are made. This is where my half brother the Jew Martin Deutcher comes in.

Oberst: How? In what way?

Hans: He is an engineer with a good knowledge of aeronautics. He will gain access to the Spitfire plant and microfilm what is needed and send us his technical assessments. As I Jew he will not be suspect. And his English is fairly good.

Oberst: And what guarantee do we have that he will not just simply as the British for Political asylum?

Hans: Simple – tomorrow he is getting married. I intend holding his wife hostage. If he does not report back regularly she will be tortured until he does contact us.

Oberst: I like it – I like it. However I still need my full quota of Jews. And I am going to be one short. Any suggestions?

Hans: I have an idea. A few days after the Jew leaves we tell his wife that he has met with a fatal accident. We draw up the death certificate which she will sign for. That will be the documentary evidence to add to your statistics.

Oberst: I must say Lieutenant your approach to problems is good. I think in future we should liaise more often.

(Fade out – Fade in to back room at the Blue Angel – a large white tablecloth is held up by Hans at one corner dressed in his Gestapo uniform, a red haired Ginger bearded Sopher at another corner. The other corners are held by two Waiters.)

Rosa: (To her Mother) How do I look Mother is my hat on straight? Do I look over dressed? And the shoes are they - -?

Mother: My darling daughter you look like what a bride should look like, happy, a little nervous. You look fine.

Rosa: You're not just saying that. Do I *really* look nice?

Mother: Why should I lie? Have I ever lied to you about anything?

Rosa: What about my father?

Mother: What about your father? When you were very young he loved us both – then a little later he found someone he loved more.

Rosa: Are all men like that? Do you think my Martin would ever–?

Mother: Rosa in a few minutes you'll be standing under the chupa. Now is not the time to have doubts.

Rosa: You are right Mother – its just nerves.

Rabbi: The Chatan is already under the Chuppa. Is the Kallah ready?

Mother: Yes we are ready.

Rabbi: Very well Mother – bring her in – lead the way.

(Mother with Rosa on her arm joins Martin under the chuppa)

Rabbi: Do we have the ring.

Martin: I couldn't get a ring. Will this brooch do?

Rabbi: Yes that's okay. Now take the brooch and give it to the Bride and repeat after me. Haray.

Martin: Haray

Rabbi: At

Martin: At

Rabbi: M'qoodeshet lee

Martin: M'qoodeshet lee

Rabbi: B' sicah zoo

Martin: B'sicah zoo

Rabbi: K'fee da-at

Martin: K'fee da-at

Rabbi: Moshe v yisrael

Martin: Moshe v yisrael.

Rabbi: Break the glass then you may kiss the bride.

(Martin does so and cries of Mazal tov are heard.
The guests make their way to the tables for a buffet tea.
Hans makes his way towards Martin and Rosa)

Hans: (Speaks to Rosa) so you are the young lady who my big brother has swept off her feet. You'll have to watch him in future. He acts first then thinks afterwards.

Rosa: He certainly moves fast. I have only known him about a day and here I am his wife.

Hans: I think Martin knows what to do most of the time. When we were little he saved me from drowning. And now he sees a charming very beautiful lady and just like that he decides to marry her.

Martin: If you two continue praising me like that my head will be so big I'll not get it through the doorposts. Mind you everything you've said about me is probably true.

Hans: Would you mind very much Rosa if I steal your gallant husband away for a short while. I need to give him some brotherly advice. I promise to bring him back shortly.

Rosa: Very well. I need to circulate among my guests.

(Rosa moves away)

Hans: Martin we have problems.

Martin: How in what way? The railways to the Channel ports are still open.

Hans: Yes – for now but for how long? There are large troop movements heading for the Polish border. War will break out at any moment. That however is the *least* of our problems. The trouble is my Superiors have found out that I am a Mischlinge.

Martin: Oh Hans – so what will happen to you? Do they know about our Mother?

Hans: They do indeed. But so far I have convinced them that Reich Marshall Goering is involved the plan.

Martin: What? And you call *me* impetuous. If they find out before you leave heaven knows what they'll do to you. And you're doing this to save me. If anything happens to you heaven forbid, I'll feel so guilty.

Hans: Look Martin what we need to do now is work out a plan.

Martin: Oh hell! There's no chance we could all stick together. Can you wangle any Gestapo transport?

Hans: I can try – what do you have in mind?

Martin: You and Rosa make for the Swiss border. If you are stopped, say that she has been arrested on suspicion of being a spy.

Hans: I'm not quite sure how that would work.

Martin: Simple – she claims to have lost her passport. That's why you are escorting her out of Germany. The last thing the Bohemian Corporal would want at this time is a diplomatic row with the Swiss.

Hans: Sounds risky – but it might just work. And what about you?

Martin: Could you get me a travel warrant?

Hans: Yes – but we'll have to move fast. You take Rosa back to your place and I'll see you there within the hour. You and Rosa leave now I'll announce to the guests that they must disperse.

[FADE OUT – FADE IN TO GESTAPO
HEADQUARTERS]

Hans: Thank you Herr Oberst. As soon as the woman is secured I shall return. Heil Hitler!

Oberst: Heil Hitler! Oh do you need a driver as well?

Hans: No Herr Oberst. I can drive and I would not wish to make any unnecessary demands on the Department at this time.

[FADE OUT – FADE IN TO MARTIN'S APARTMENT]

Martin: Well Hans how did it go – did you have much trouble?

Hans: No – and that's what's bothering me.

Rosa: Why – what's wrong?

Hans: Look out the window and try not to be seen.

Martin: I'm looking.

Hans: Is there a military vehicle with three or four soldiers in it.

Martin: No I can't – wait a bit – yes there is one drawing up now.

Hans: let me know where it parks.

Martin: its going slowly passed – hang on – it's reversing – it's stopped right opposite the Apartment building.

Hans: Let me see – ah ha – yes it's the one that tailed me here. The chances are they are spying on me. So this is what we need to do. Martin the apartment below – is it occupied?

Martin: No it's been empty for months.

Hans: Is there any way you can get in without asking the Consigner for the key?

Martin: I don't see how – he has the key to – oh now then – if I remember rightly the entrance lock was faulty which is why I took this flat instead. I'm pretty sure the lock has not yet been repaired.

Hans: Very well – in that case we must move fast – you two say your goodbyes. I'll be in the hallway. Please don't be long.

Rosa: (Embraces Hans – they kiss) Oh Martin will we ever see each other again?

Martin: I hope so my sherne gelipta Rosa. Tell you what I'll always wear my half of the twin brooches I bought you and you wear yours always.

Rosa: If there was some way we could –

Martin: - All we can do now is hope and pray.

Hans: (Bursts in) Sorry to interrupt – we must move. Martin you wait till you see both vehicles move off. Then go out via the fire escape from the flat below. Rosa I'll put these handcuffs on you – goodbye brother best of luck.

Rosa: Goodbye my Knight in shining armour – till we meet again.

Martin: (Forcing back tears) Bye my sherne gelipte.

(FADE OUT – FADE IN TO HANS AND ROSA)

Hans: Look in the wing mirror – are they still following?

Rosa: Yes they are keeping up. When do you think they'll try arrest us?

Hans: They won't get the chance if all goes to plan? There's the radio switch near your left hand – switch it on please. There maybe some news.

Rosa: (operates the switch) Wagner is my favourite –

Voice: On Radio: We interrupt this programme with the following announcement. In order to protect Germans living in Poland our glorious armed forces have crossed in to Poland. The Reich has been threatened that if our forces do not cease their protective action to save German lives – a state of war will be declared on the Reich by the British Empire. The Fuhrer refuses to be intimidated by these threats. Stay tuned to your radios and await instructions – in the –

Hans: Switch it off please Rosa. We all knew it was coming. The war has begun.

Rosa: I hope Martin is okay. Do you think he will have caught the train in time? (Cries bitterly)

Martin: (reassuringly) I'm sure he would have done. That's one thing my big brother has in common with Herr Hitler.

Rosa: (With a forced smile) Oh yes and what's that.

Hans: They both love precision *and* Punctuality. If Herr Hitler says the train will leave at 20.15 my big brother will be at the station at 20.14. This means that the train will be now very close to the French border, if not actually in France.

Rosa: I do so hope you are right Hans.

Hans: Can you still see our pursuers?

Rosa: I can – just. I think we are losing them. Oh I think they are stopping.

Hans: I'll just pull up over there. Rosa feel under your seat. My binoculars are there.

Rosa: (Passes binocular case to Hans) they are very heavy.

Hans: And very powerful. Now let me see. One of them has gone into the Post Office we just passed. I don't like this Rosa.

Rosa: Why – what's wrong?

Hans: The soldiers are setting up a road block and the Officer is going inside.

Rosa: But we are not going back in there direction. Why should-?

Hans: Take a look ahead. There is a Police road block forming.

Rosa: (Nervously) what shall we do? I'm frightened!

Hans: Well there are no side roads. We must go straight on – Here goes.

(The car goes forward and is hailed down by a Policeman)

Hans: Problems Officer?

Policeman: Papers if you please sir.

(Hans passes his documents to the Policeman who examines the very closely. He looks up at Hans and stares at Rosa. He beckons to a more Senior Policeman who runs over quickly. He grabs Hans's documents. A few seconds later he looks up)

Senior Policeman: I must ask you and the prisoner to come with me. Switch off your engine and give me the Keys please sir.

(Hans notices that the Gestapo vehicle that followed them has closed up. He motions to Rosa to step out of the car. He exits via the driver's door.)

Hans: Where now Officer?

Senior Policeman: Just follow me. It's not far.

(Rosa is escorted by two Policemen. The Gestapo personnel follow. After walking about a hundred yards or so they arrive at a Police Station. They enter an imposing looking office where a Senior Police Officer is seated behind a large desk. He introduces himself to Hans.)

Superintendent: Good evening Lieutenant Zimmerschaft I am Superintendent Schmitt. (He picks up the phone receiver) Get me the duty Oberst at Gestapo Headquarters Bad Hertzberg. (He addresses Rosa's Police guards) Take the woman next door and wait till I call you. Good evening Herr Oberst – Yes he is here now – very well just one moment. (Passes the receiver to Hans)

Hans: Good evening Herr Oberst

Oberst: Good evening Lieutenant – There has been a change in our plan. High Command is not entirely happy with our schedules. You must now obtain the signature of Frau Rosa Deutcher.

Hans: But Herr Oberst – that was our original plan – why is it different.

Oberst: The difference is Lieutenant is – both you and the lady will return here under escort, and the document will be signed in the presence of the Police Superintendent who will witness the signature.

Hans: Very good Herr Oberst – as you say Heil Hitler (Replaces the receiver and Produces the Fake Death certificate and places it on the desk.

Superintendent: Bring in the woman.

(Rosa is escorted in – she looks pale and distraught)

Superintendent: (Addresses Rosa) you may be seated. Are you Rosa Deutcher who was illegally married yesterday?

Rosa: I *was* married yesterday but I swear I had no idea it was illegal.

Superintendent: No matter – the Lieutenant has something to tell you.

Hans: Rosa – I have just been speaking with my Headquarters – they informed me that Martin was involved in an accident.

Rosa: Accident – What sort of accident? Is he alright?

Hans: Please keep calm – you must be brave and strong.

Rosa: (Becoming hysterical) He's dead isn't he? I know it – How did it happen? Where -?

Hans: Please Rosa try to stay calm. The full circumstances are not yet clear. It seems the Police were chasing some criminals and as they fired Martin was caught in the crossfire. As you can see from this Death Certificate – it says accidental death. I'd like you to sign it and keep a copy the Superintendent will –

Rosa: (Still Hysterical) Death Certificate – Where did you get it? How could-

Hans: Please Rosa – I know you are shocked – the truth is my Headquarters dictated the details over the telephone to the Superintendent which is why he must countersign it to verify the details.

Superintendent: If you would please sign Frau Deutcher – I am very busy.

Rosa: (Sniffing and panting as she calms down, she signs the document) so that's it then! That's all I have to show for my marriage. I've no future just the memory of a beautiful dream. My happiness is at an end. (Bursts into tears again).

Hans: Come Rosa we have to –

(At that moment the wail of an air-raid siren is heard)

Superintendent: Everybody to the Shelters. This is only a practice. You all know where to go. Come On move! Move! Move!

Hans: Where shall we go?

Superintendent: Anywhere – but get out of here – now.

Hans: Rosa quick (He grabs her arm)

Rosa: (doe fully) Where to – as though it matters to me now my life is finished.

Hans: No time grief now Rosa. Just stick by me. Look over there. Let's mingle with the crowd. They must be going to a shelter.

(They find themselves in a crowded shelter that is dimly lit.)

A Voice: Hans! Hans Zimmerschaft is that you?

Hans: Hello who is that I don't recognise – By all that's wonderful Greta what are you doing her?

Greta: Maybe I should be asking you that question and what are you doing in the Gestapo?

Hans: It's a long story. Oh by the way this is Rosa. Rosa meet my cousin Greta.

Greta: Hello Rosa (to Hans) is she alright?

Hans: Another long story – she's had a shock. (In a whisper) the truth is she has to get out of Germany – any ideas.

Greta: Sure – I was driving my truck back to Emmen when the air raid practice sounded.

Hans: How long have you been living in Holland?

Greta: Nearly seven years. Father and I sell Dutch cheeses here and we take German goods into Holland.

Hans: Can you hide Rosa in the back of your truck?

Greta: Sure – I always give the Border guards some cheese and they let me through.

Hans: Rosa you go with Greta – it's your only chance.

Rosa: But what about you? You are my only connection with Martin and now I'm to loose you as well – It's just not fair.

(THE ALL CLEAR SOUNDS AND EVRYONE MAKES
THEIR WAY OUT OF THESHELTER)

Hans: Bye Rosa – Bye Greta. Maybe one day well see each other again.

Rosa: (embraces Hans and kisses him) I'll never forget your kindness Hans – never.

Hans: Go now both of you. (To himself) I hope you never find out how I lied to you.

· ·

(IT IS NOW 1948 IN NEW YORK – AN ART, TEACHER
ROSA IS TEACHING AT A GIRLS ART SCHOOL. THE
SCENE OPENS WITH A VIEW INTO A CLASSROOM.
BY THE ENTRANCE DOOR TWO ELDERLY WOMEN
ARE LOOKING AND LISTENING.)

Rosa: Welcome to my class young ladies. I hope you will regard me as a friend and not just a teacher. They call me Rosa Smith – you may call me Miss Smith or Miss Rosa – whatever makes you feel comfortable.

Jane Taylor: (She and Miriam Feld – the school principle – move toward the Principle's office.) She seems to have a nice manner. Where is she from? How long has she been here?

Miriam Feld: (Opens door to her office) after you Mrs.Taylor please take a seat. In answer to your questions, Miss Smith came here just after the war. All I know about her is that she is a Jewish refugee from Nazi Germany. She never speaks about her past. All that concerns me is that she gets on well with all her pupils. Even those who have left still keep in contact with her.

Jane Taylor: So maybe she could help my granddaughter Diane.

Miriam Feld: I cannot guarantee anything you understand. However according to what you wrote in your letter I see no reason why your granddaughter shouldn't gain something from her time here. There's one thing that does bother me slightly.

Jane Taylor: Tell me – what's the matter.

Miriam Feld: You mentioned in your letter – just a second I have it here – 'Her father wants nothing to do with her – the Mental Care Team say this is the basis of her problems.' – could you elaborate?

Jane Taylor: It's a real tragedy. My son-in-law and daughter were married for just two years. She fell pregnant after fifteen months. Everything was going okay the there was a complication. It was a case of who to save – the mother or the baby – or lose both of them.

Miriam Feld: So who had to make the decision?

Jane Taylor: It should have been the father – but for some reason they couldn't get hold of him. There wasn't enough time to go searching – it was that desperate.

Miriam Feld: Oh dear – so who in the end decided?

Jane Taylor: The Doctor – He was a staunch Catholic and by them in such cases the new life is more important than the mother's life.

Miriam Feld: How awful – I can imagine how your son-in-law reacted.

Jane Taylor: With great respect Mrs. Feld you *can't* imagine – believe me *nobody* could imagine. My son-in-law could have ended up in jail. He threatened the Doctor's life. Anyway – to cut a long story short – he wouldn't have anything to do with the baby. To this day he hasn't set eyes on her (Begins to sob) he says she is responsible for killing his wife.

Miriam Feld: (Passes a tissue) Here dry your eyes – So has there been any contact between you and Diane's father.

Jane Taylor: The last time was about five years ago. I had to stop my husband from hitting him. What an argument! You should never know such bitterness. My husband called him all the low down selfish stupid evil scum on the face of the earth. I tried to explain that we also grieve for my daughter.

Miriam Feld: Well of course you do after all you knew her all her life. He knew her – how long – two three years.

Jane Taylor: Exactly – that's what made my husband – bless him – so angry. I know it my sound strange – but the truth is Dave – my son-in-law absolutely idolised my Diana – if anything too much – He couldn't enough for her – every month another expensive piece of jewellery – whether he could afford it or not.

Miriam Feld: It seems to me your son-in-law is one of those intense people who cannot control his passions. It sounds as though he is shutting out his daughter in order to keep up his hatred of the Doctor.

Jane Taylor: You know what Mrs. Feld my husband said those self same words. Exactly the same.

Miriam Feld: So how did you manage to tell your granddaughter about the situation? You must forgive me for asking such pertinent questions. You see we get all sorts of girls here from – what can I say – unusual backgrounds and the Staff need to know how to handle them. You know what I mean.

Jane Taylor: Of course I understand. When Diane was about nine she asked about her mother and father. We told her that her mother had passed away and her father had an important job with Government which meant he was always travelling.

Miriam Feld: Did she ever wonder why he never phoned or wrote?

Jane Taylor: We told her that his work was hush hush and where he was had to be kept secret.

Miriam Feld: And when did she find out the truth?

Jane Taylor: It was – what maybe – just over two years ago. She sensed something wasn't right. I don't know if she'd been talking to her school friends or what. Anyway we spoke to our Rabbi and all he could say is we should pray and remember just how sensitive the issue was – as though we were a couple of Schmiggegs. So we asked if he or the Rebbitzen would speak to her.

Miriam Feld: Sounds like a good idea to me. They have training in that sort of thing.

Jane Taylor: Naturally that's what we thought. They didn't want to know. He said it would be better coming from us. I tell you one thing – he knows how to drink scotch at simchas. Anyhow my husband decided that he would tell her. I'll never forget as I live the look of sadness and tears in her eyes – I held her so tight in my arms.

Miriam Feld: (Looks at letter) I see from your letter you say she became totally withdrawn and you took her to the Mental Health Team.

Jane Taylor: And now I'm here. You are our only hope.

Miriam Feld: Bring Diane here tomorrow about ten. We'll do our best.

Jane Taylor: That's all anyone can do (Sighs deeply)

(FADE OUT – FADE IN TO CLASSROOM)

Rosa: Come in Diane – everyone stop what you are doing for a moment – This is Diane who will be joining us for the rest of the term. Diane where would you like to sit?

Diane: Where ever there is room.

Rosa: Sit next to Myrna. Myrna show Diane where all the paints are the rest of you carry on and I'll look at each painting.

Myrna: Hi Diane would you like to look at what I'm doing?

Diane: (In a sullen tone) sure – why not I suppose it makes no difference.

Myrna: (Taken aback) well – what this is – is a painting about feelings. Miss Rosa asked us to paint how we feel most of the time and when we are sad and happy.

Diane: (Looks closely at the painting) which is which?

Myrna: I think all the red spots and the white stripes are my happy moods and the dark colours are when I'm unhappy.

Diane: My daddy thinks I killed my mother. Do you think I could do that?

Myrna: (Taken aback) why would he think that?

Diane: I think its something to do with what happened when I was born.

Myrna: Can't you just ask him?

Diane: No – I've never met him

Myrna: I – I don't know what to say. Tell you what let's speak to Miss Rosa she's lovely. She understands a lot. Shall I call her over?

Diane: Sure – I just feel so bad all the time. Am I really so awful? I've never wanted to harm anyone.

Myrna: Of course you're not bad. – Miss Rosa can you come here please?

Rosa: (Walks over smiling) Are you two getting on okay? How's the painting coming on?

Myrna: The painting is – well so so – its Diane Miss she is very unhappy. Her father hates her.

Rosa: (very softly) Diane – I want you to paint how you feel. (She embraces Diane and Myrna) Would you two like to come to my flat after school for tea? We'll be able to talk better there.

Myrna: Wow Miss Rosa that'll be just great. I'll phone my dad and let him know. Isn't that at great Diane?

Diane: I'm not sure – I never go out much and besides I'll have to ask my Grandma.

Rosa: I'm sure your grandma will let you come. Tell you what I'll phone her from the Principle's office. You two carry on painting I'll be back shortly.

(FADE OUT = FADE IN TO PRINCIPLE'S OFFICE)

Miriam Feld: (On phone) I don't mind telling you Mrs Taylor I've never known a pupil to open up so quickly. (Longish pause) That's right although the next stage is critical I'm sure Miss Smith will bring her back to normal. (Short pause) and you Mrs. Taylor bye for now. (Replaces Receiver) Well Rosa once again you've been a great help.

Rosa: The truth is Principle, Diane opened up right away with Myrna.

Miriam Feld: I must say Rosa the school appreciates the fact you are giving up your free time to help our pupils. You are very kind.

Rosa: If I'm honest – I don't go out on an evening and somehow I feel close to Diane and Myrna. In fact I'm looking forward to it.

(FADE OUT – FADE IN TO ROSA'S FLAT –
ALL THREE ARE LOOKING AT ROSA'S PAINTINGS
AND DRINKING COFFEE)

Myrna: I like this one Miss Rosa. The bright reds then the heavy blacks and I love the way the reddish pinks blend.

Rosa: Tell me what do you think it means?

Myrna: In what way Miss Rosa?

Rosa: How can I put this? Describe the artist's feelings. What do you think is the basic personality of the artist? Have you any ideas Diane?

Diane: I think the artist had something that he loved very much. Then the heavy black shows that he lost it or maybe had it taken away and the reddish pinks with blacks mean that he wants to find what he'd lost but doesn't know where to find it.

Myrna: I just see a confused person who doesn't want to accept disappointment and that's why the artist always has an aching heart. Who is the artist Miss Rosa – do you know him?

Rosa: (Smiles broadly) the artist is not a him – all pictures you see are mine. I am the artist.

Myrna: Oh Miss Rosa I'm so sorry – I hope you don't think I was speaking out of turn.

Rosa: Of course not Myrna – your interpretation was accurate. So was yours Diane. In fact if you two study and practice you could be both be really good artists.

Diane: I'll never be good at anything. I'm sure my father wouldn't have sent me away if were a good person. Maybe I was born bad.

Rosa: Now you listen to me Diane and listen very carefully. Nobody is born bad or good or anything like that. We are mainly the way we are because of or experiences.

Diane: I wish I could believe that. I know I don't want to be evil – but I don't know why my father cast me away (Cries bitterly).

Myrna: (Embraces Diane) please Diane don't think that way – look how quickly you became my friend. Am I not right Miss Rosa?

Rosa: I think the time has come for someone to speak to Diane's father. But first of all another cup of coffee all round.

(FADE OUT – FADE IN TO PRICIPLE'S OFFICE)

Rosa: That's what happened. So if you can let me have Mr. Kopperman's work address – I'll go and speak with him.

Miriam Feld: (Passes a paper with all the details) are you sure this is the best way to deal with this?

Rosa: Madam Principle – most of my life has been ruined by cruel bullies – by men who enjoy inflicting pain on others. Now I am going to hit back. It is too late for me – but there's still time for my pupil Diane.

Miriam Feld: I hope you know what you are doing Rosa. You know in all the years I've known you this is the first time you've mentioned your past.

Rosa: My past is something I want to forget – except for – (Breaks off and a tear falls)

Miriam Feld: Rosa if you should feel like talking about it – my door is always open.

Rosa: (Smiles) thank you – I'll get on my way.

Miriam Feld: (Takes money out of a petty cash box) Here take a cab. Best of luck.

(FADE OUT – FADE IN ROSA LEAVES TAXI AND LOOKS UP AT BUILDING – LOOKS AT NOTE AND READS –DAVID KOPPERMAN ADVERTISEING EXCEUTIVE – TOWERADS AGENCEY 19 SECOND AVENUE – THIRD STREET. SHE ENTERS THE BUILDING AND TAKES ELEVATOR TO FOURTH FLOOR. GOES TO RECEPTION DESK)

Receptionist: Good Morning I'm Angela how may I help you?

Rosa: I must speak with Mr. David Kopperman it's very urgent.

Receptionist: Mr. Kopperman is in conference right now. He should be finished within the hour.

Rosa: (Looks round at the markings on the doors. She sees one marked 'Conference Room' Sorry this is urgent (Strides over purposefully to the Conference Room)

Receptionist: (Gets up from her desk) I'm sorry but you can't go in there. Please –

Rosa: Watch me! (Opens door and looks at the four men and two women seated there. She notices a name plate in front of a man who looked very attractive. She gasps then regains her posture and in a loud voice) Mr. Kopperman why did you accuse your daughter of committing murder when you no that is a malicious evil lie?

(ALL PRESENT ARE TAKEN ABACK THERE IS A FEW SECONDS SHOCKED SILENCE)

Dave Kopperman: (Bewildered and agitated) Lady I don't know who you are and what you are doing here but if you don't leave now I'll have you thrown out.

Rosa: If you do that then I'll go straight to the New York Times office then on to the Jewish Press and tell them how you've caused your daughter to have a mental breakdown. I don't think the publicity will do this firm a lot of good – do you?

Chairman: Dave – show this lady into your office – sort out what ever the matter is – we'll resume this meeting after lunch. Oh and Dave – When I say sort – I do mean sort.

Dave Kopperman: Leave it to me Chief – (Turns to Rosa) Okay lady follow me.

(They exit the Conference Room –
cross the Reception area and enter Dave's office)

Receptionist: I'm sorry Mr. Kopperman – I explained that –

Dave Kopperman: Its okay – (Dave and Rosa enter Dave's office) Okay lady – sit down please and tell me just what the hell is going on?

Rosa: To start with Mr.Kopperman you will moderate your language when speaking to me. Then you will do me the courtesy of listening to what I have to say.

Dave Kopperman: Madame you have the audacity and Chutzpah to burst into my firm accuse me in front of my colleagues of being some sort of criminal – and *you* expect *me* to be polite and courteous? Very well just tell me what's bothering you.

Rosa: What's bothering me Mr.Kopperman is you. You have a beautiful talented daughter who believes she is a bad person. Her self confidence is non-existent and all because her selfish cruel father has a twisted evil sense of values. (Glares at Dave – but the more she looks at him the she is attracted to him) Do you understand what I'm talking about? Or don't you care?

Dave: Quite frankly Mrs (Pauses)

Rosa: Smith – *Miss* Smith

Dave: Quite frankly Miss Smith I do not see why I should have to answer you about my family. Please explain just exactly who you are and what you are after.

Rosa: I'm the Senior Art Teacher at a school for Jewish girls who come from broken homes. It may not occur to you Mr. Kopperman that although your daughter is well loved and looked after by her grandparents, the fact she knows her father hates her is causing her deep mental stress. The only way her illness can be cured is for her to come close to her father. (An uncomfortable pause – Rosa notices Dave's eyes glazing over. He buries his head in his hands)

Dave: Miss Smith in the Conference Room you blurted out in front of everyone that I thought my daughter was a murderess. That was a cruel thing to say. Why did you do It.?

Rosa: For the same reason you cast Diane aside. Revenge. You wanted to destroy the Doctor who in your eyes killed your wife. And *I* wanted revenge on all those evil people who destroyed *my* happiness. So you see we are both two of a kind – and now we are even.

Dave: So they named her Diane – my wife's name was Diana – (He tries to hold back his tears).

Rosa: I didn't know that.

Dave: I miss my wife so much. Would you believe me if I told you I never been with another woman since I lost her. Please don't mention it to anyone but I still cry every night – I cannot ever forget her. Heaven alone knows why I'm telling you this.

Rosa: The reason is Mr.Kopperman –

Dave: Please call me Dave. All my friends call me Dave.

Rosa: The reason why you've opened up to me is like I said we are two of a kind. Tell me Dave just how long did you know your wife?

Dave: It was just over a year before we decided to marry. She was so kind. Had the sought of voice and hair that most men dream about. I fell deeply in love – and if the truth be known – I'm still in love with her.

Rosa: So all in all your relationship lasted three whole years. Dave let me show you something I have not shown to anybody. (Opens her briefcase and withdraws two documents). You see this document.

Dave: That's a Ketuba

Rosa: Yes it's mine – see the date – not the Hebrew – second September 1939. Now look at *this* document.

(FLASHBACK)
. . . . . The Death Certificate reads Accidental death . . . .

Dave: (Looks blank) you mean your husband was *killed* the day after your wedding? (Longish pause) And how long had you know each other *before* the wedding?

Rosa: About twenty- four hours. You see Dave all I have to show for my Marriage is a wedding certificate, a Death certificate and this (She unpins the brooch from her lapel. This is what my Husband gave to me under the chupah. I hope now you can understand why I felt so harshly toward you. Three whole years of Marriage and a very beautiful daughter – by the way looking at you I can see where she gets her good looks from.

Dave: I thank you for the compliment – did you ever meet another man you might want to –

Rosa: Dave you are not the only one who cries himself to sleep at night.

Dave: Rosa do you think you could arrange for me to meet Diane. Trouble is what could I say to her?

Rosa: (Takes an envelope form her brief case and hands it to Dave) Diane asked me to give you this.

Dave: Do you know what's in it?

Rosa: No – would you like to read it in private I can wait outside.

Dave: No stay, please stay – would you read it for me.

Rosa: Let's compromise – I'll stay if you read it aloud.

Dave: Very well (He opens the envelope – and begins to read) Dear Daddy I so much want see you and prove to you that I'm not really (Stops reading and cries profusely – Rosa walks over to him and puts her arm around his shoulders.

Rosa: It's alright Dave – just pause a second the continue it'll help

Dave: (Continues reading) . . I'm not really a bad person. Please – Please say you'll come. I'm so very unhappy. Your Daughter Diane. Will you make the arrangements Rosa? I'm confused, guilty. I'm going to need a lot of help.

Rosa: Are you free tomorrow say about four-o-clock?

Dave: You bet.

Rosa: (Hands him a card) that's where I live. I'll prepare some tea and then go out somewhere so you can be alone with Diane.

Dave: Would it be possible for you to be on hand? I'm bound to get tongue-tied and maybe she won't like me.

Rosa: You know what Dave – maybe I'll do just that. It will give me some practice being in the company of a very handsome man.

Dave: (Smiles and blushes faintly) It's a long time since I enjoyed the company of a charming interesting lady.

Rosa: (Smiles and chuckles) so you don't think I'm beautiful.

Dave: Rosa you know I'm an Advertising executive. I cannot tell a lie. Mind you sometimes I have been known to hide the truth. Oh and there's something else – How should I open up to her?

Rosa: Open up? I'm not sure what you mean. Is it the first thing to say or maybe –?

Dave: Well no not really. Should I bring her a gift? I realise even a present can't compensate for the lost years – but I can't just come empty handed.

Rosa: A bouquet of flowers would be a great help. Nothing *too* big but not small. Oh and a nice piece of jewellery. I can tell you her favourite colour is Turquoise so a Sapphire necklace might just do the trick.

Dave: That was her mother's favourite colour too. If only it could have been an uncomplicated birth. What a wonderful family we would have made.

Rosa: Make sure you tell her that – and how much she reminds you of her.

Dave: I suppose I'll have a job making peace with my former In-Laws. How on earth am I going to meet that hurdle?

Rosa: One step at a time Dave. It'll probably take much longer but you never know.

Dave: I've made such a mess of things – if only I could put the clock back.

Rosa: It's the future that matters now Dave. Mind you I'm not the one who should be saying that to you. At night all I do is sit and dream about what might have been.

Dave: I think in your case Rosa it *is* understandable. Oh by the way there is something about the dates on the documents you just showed. Yet I can't put my finger on it.

Rosa: I'll give you a clue Dave, the dates my life changed for ever were the first and second of September 1939. Can you remember what happened on the third of September?

Dave: Yes it familiar now what—*of course* the out break of war. What a shmiggegg I am – in more ways that one. After what you've been through I feel even more stupid than I did before. It's been one big mess.

Rosa: Well all that's behind you now Dave. No point in raking it all up.

Dave: (With a deep sigh) so until tomorrow then.

Rosa: Until tomorrow. You have my number. Bye (exits)

Dave: Bye Rosa – and thank you so much.

(FADE OUT – FADE IN TO ROSA'S CLASSROOM
THE FOLLOWING MORING)

Rosa: This morning ladies we will discuss each of your paintings. As I call your name bring your work to the front easel and in a few sentences state the title and explain the theme. Sandra you first please. Diane please step outside for a moment I need to speak with you. Sandra please carry on.

(ROSA AND DIANE LEAVE THE ROOM)

Rosa: (Takes both of Diane's hands) I have some very good news. Guess who is coming to tea with us this afternoon?

Diane: You mean – really my Daddy read my letter? I can't believe it. Did he really, really say he wanted to (Begins to sob softly) to see me.

Rosa: (With a smile and a laugh) Oh yes he most certainly is coming.

Diane: Oh Miss Rosa – How did you –

Rosa: No more questions. I think perhaps you should go home now and maybe wear the dress you like the best. Will your Grandma be home now?

Diane: Yes – Thursday she prepares the meals for Shabbos. I help her after school. (Eyes glazing over) my daddy is coming to see me. I hope every thing will be alright.

Rosa: I'm sure it will. I can tell you he wants to meet you as much as you want meet him. And not only is that he just as nervous as you are. (She laughs).

(FADE OUT – FADE IN TO THE
TAYLOR'S APARTMENT)

Jane Taylor: Is that you Sam? You're home early.

Rosa: No Grandma it's me Diane.

Jane Taylor: Diane what's happened – why so early – has something happened in school?

Diane: Grandma you'll never guess what, never, never, never.

Jane Taylor: Why so much excitement Diane? Don't tell me one of your paintings is going for exhibition. Your Grandpa always said one day you'd be a great Artist.

Diane: No Grandma – it's something much better.

Jane Taylor: I don't understand what could be so much better than that?

Diane: I'm having tea with Miss Rosa and (In a high pitch voice) *My Daddy is coming as well*

Jane Taylor: Gevalt – Der groyse schvance of a lobus has decided to visit his daughter. Siz a clog Tzu dem yahren.

Diane: Are you angry Grandma – I don't understand any Yiddish.

Jane Taylor: No Diane – not so much angry – as a little shocked. If you're pleased then I'm happy for you believe me am I happy. I'm not so sure how your Grandpa will react. When, all being well you see your Father – you can tell him from me that *punctuality* is taki a real virtue.

Diane: Punctuality Grandma? – I don't understand.

Jane Taylor: Take my word for it Diane your *father* will understand. I just hope your Grandfather will not go meshugge when I tell him the news. In the meantime sit down I'll make you some lunch.

(FADE OUT – FADE IN TO ROSA'S FLAT)

Rosa: Remember Diane – when your father comes in – just stand up and wait for him to come to you let him speak first. And it's possible he will start crying. Don't be put off – men sometimes do cry.

(THE DOOR BELL RINGS)

Diane: Oh dear I feel so nervous (Starts to tremble)

Rosa: Sit down – take three deep breaths – are you Okay?

Diane: I think so

Rosa: (Goes to the door – opens it and says in a whisper) hello Dave follow me. (In a normal voice) Mr.Kopperman may I present your daughter Diane.

(DIANE STANDS UP – DAVE STANDS AND
STARES HE APPROACHES DIANE VERY SLOWLY)

Dave: These flowers are for you Diane. I hope you like flowers.

Diane: These flowers are the most beautiful I've ever seen.

Rosa: Here let me take them. I'll just go into the kitchen and find a vase for them. (Takes the bouquet and leaves)

Dave: (Eyes welling up with tears) I read your letter Diane and I just want to sat that (Pauses) that I (Chokes up goes forward embraces Diane and cries profusely on her neck and shoulders).

Diane (Full of tears) I'm so glad you came daddy.

(ENTER ROSA – CARRYING A TRAY TEA AND CAKES)

Rosa: Who is ready for Pecan pie or perhaps chocolate cake with their tea?

Dave: Can't resist chocolate cake. (Sniffs and wipes eyes)

Rosa: I know Diane loves Pecan pie.

Dave: Just like her mother. We always had a good stock of it in the Apartment.

Diane: What else did she like daddy? Grandma and Grandpa don't like talking about her.

Dave: I could go on talking about her all night. She had the same colouring skin as yours Diane. Her hair was just like yours too.

Diane: Did she like art at all?

Dave: She read a lot. Mainly Romantic fiction. Oh and music. Nearly all our dates were visits to the Opera and sometimes the Ballet. What about you Diane? Do you like music?

Diane: Sometimes – I love drawing and painting.

Dave: Of course – Miss Rosa told me you were a keen student. (Puts his hand in his inside pocket – and withdraws a presentation case) I have been told that Turquoise is your favourite colour. Is that right Diane?

Diane: I like it the best yes that's right.

Dave: If that's the case – I somehow think you'll like this. (He hands her the presentation case)

Diane: For me!

Dave: For you – go on open it.

Diane: (Opens the box very slowly – she gasps at the sapphire on a gold chained necklace with matching ear rings.) How beautiful – look Miss Rosa I never had anything like this ever.

Rosa: Here let me put it on for you. There's a mirror in the bedroom.

(Diane exits – Rosa turns to Dave)

Dave: How am I doing Rosa? I still feel a bit strange. I keep thinking where will she live. Should I ask her to be with me or should she-

Rosa: One step at a time Dave. I am sure her depression will disappear now that you have come in to her life. Perhaps –

(Diane bursts in)

Diane: Isn't this just perfect? It's wonderful. Thanks Daddy so much. I think though I'd better save up for a new dress to match it properly.

Dave: That's the sort of remark your mother used to make each time I bought her some jewellery. Something tells me Diane that you and I should go on a shopping trip.

Diane: Oh when daddy when?

Dave: That depends on your schedule. What do you do at weekends?

Diane: Sometimes I go to Synagogue with Grandpa. Sunday depends on the weather.

Dave: I'd better have a word with Sam and Jane. Do they know about our meeting?

Diane: Yes – I told Grandma and she said some words in Yiddish that I didn't understand – oh and then she said I should tell daddy something about being punctual. She said you'd understand.

Dave: (Smiles at both of them) Now that is typical of your grandma. She can tell you off and disguise it with humour. She's a real lady.

Rosa: I'm not quite sure I understand.

Dave: She didn't say where were you for fourteen years. She just said punctuality is a good thing.

Rosa: As you say Dave Diane's Grandmother sounds quite a lady.

Dave: I suppose I'd better have a word with them. The sooner the better. When will Your Grandpa be home Diane?

Diane: I'm not sure. Sometimes he plays chess at his club on a Thursday and he doesn't get back till late. I wonder should I phone home and ask?

Rosa: Use the phone in the hall. But don't tell them your father will be with you.

Diane: Why not Miss Rosa?

Rosa: Trust me Diane. I am sure that if they know your father wants to visit they will say no. Let it be a surprise. Tell you what I'll go with you.

(FADE OUT – FADE IN TO THE TAYLOR APPARTMENT ENTRANCE DOOR DIANE PRESSES THE BUZZER)

Jane Taylor: (Shouts out) who is it?

Diane: It's me Grandma. I brought some friends.

Jane Taylor: (Opens the doors) Hello come in Miss Rosa isn't it? I recognise you from (Her eyes alight on Dave) so finally at long last you've seen sense. I can't say I'm overjoyed – and when Sam gets back he'll probably go berserk – You'd better come in for Diane's sake.

Dave: Look Mrs. Taylor – I don't expect –

Jane Taylor: What's with the Mrs. Taylor all of a sudden you've forgotten my name in fourteen years. Not enough you should forget your daughter. Since when does unhappiness cause amnesia? (Turns to Diane) Diane maybe you could show Miss Rosa the Kitchen and make a little snack for us yes.

Diane: This way Miss Rosa – sharn't be long daddy.

Jane Taylor: Take your time Diane (Turns to Dave.) You know Dave you were a good husband to my daughter and good son-in-law to me and Sam. Didn't it enter your head that *we* needed our good son-in-law after what happened? We could have helped each other. We –

(THE ENTRANCE DOOR OPENS)

Sam Taylor: Only me shayndele your wonderful Hus—(He sees Dave)

Dave: Good evening Mr. Taylor – before you say anything – I know it sounds inadequate but I'm truly very sorry for all the tzoress I've caused you and Mrs. Taylor.

Sam Taylor: Oh very nice wonderful. You come in here and you are very sorry. Did you here that Jane? *He* is sorry for the trouble that *he* has caused *us*. About his daughter who he neglected from the moment she was born he says *nothing*. Gornit not a word – very nice ---

Jane Taylor: Sam – listen up a second. Dave has made sholem with Diane. I know how you feel but we've got to look forward.

Sam Taylor: I am sorry Jane – for me it's not that easy. For years I struggled to make a living. My lovely daughter was taken from us and did we get any support from the one person who could have helped us through the heartache? No all he does is think about him. Not a single thought about you or me. No he turns his back on his daughter – did he sit Shiva? No – not even *one single* Kaddish.

Jane Taylor: Sam – Diane is here in the kitchen with her teacher Miss Rosa. I don't want a bad atmosphere Sam. Are you listening to me Sam?

Sam Taylor: So who's making a bad atmosphere? I'm not the one who neglected his responsibilities and left a load of trouble and tzoress for his daughter and family. And what's more I'm not the cause of my grand-daughter's depression. So why accuse *me* of making a bad atmosphere?

Dave: (In a sullen voice) I think I should leave. All I ask is ---

Jane Taylor: No Dave you *will not* leave. *I* insist that you stay. As for you Sam Taylor – now *you* are behaving like Dave did for all these years. At least Dave is trying to make amends. And what are you doing? Sam for Diane's sake at least be civil to Dave. (In a soft tone) Come on Sam deep down you know I'm right.

Sam Taylor: (Takes a deep breath) you know Dave not to have any contact. Not even a birthday card – that's what hurt the most.

Dave: Look Mr. Taylor I –

Sam Taylor: Dave there was a time when you called us Sam and Jane. So forget the Mr. Taylor business.

Dave: Well Sam I just wanted to say if the positions were reversed I'd be just like you – I doubt if I could have made Sholem. I cannot undo the past but I can try for the future.

Jane Taylor: I'll see what's happening in the kitchen. You'll stay for dinner Dave.

Dave: That would be very nice. (His eyes glaze over – his voice falters) I remember the first time I had dinner here. After coffee Sam and I had our first game of chess. Do you remember Sam?

Sam Taylor: (In a soft voice) Not only do I remember – I recorded the moves. I still have it somewhere. You played awful because your attention was elsewhere.

Dave: (Takes out a handkerchief – wipes eyes) my attention is *still* elsewhere Sam. I think about her every day *and* night.

Sam Taylor: Know what Dave – I think we should have a game after dinner.

Dave: I'd like that Sam. It's so nice being in this apartment again, it brings back so many happy memories. I never thought I could ever recall such happiness.

Sam Taylor: Ah Here come the ladies. What's for dinner?

(FADE OUT – FADE IN – TO END OF MEAL – DAVE
AND SAM ARE PLAYING CHESS AT ONE END OF
THE L SHAPED ROOM. THE LADIES ARE DRINKING
COFFEE. IT IS NEARLY 10.00P.M.)

Diane: I'm feeling very tired – I must go to bed. I'll say good night to Grandpa and daddy. (When out of ear shot)

Jane Taylor: You've done a wonderful job with Diane. She's never been so happy. Are so involved with all your pupils?

Rosa: I've had a few successes. Some not so successful. So far as Diane is concerned – it's you and Mr. Taylor who did all the work. I just followed on.

Jane Taylor: Tell me Rosa – woman to woman – how did you manage to get through to Dave

Rosa: (Smiles) well Mrs. Taylor it was –

Jane Taylor: its Jane and Sam – forget the Mr. and Mrs. Carry on with the story.

Rosa: Very well – Jane – I went to Dave's office and (FLASHBACK) .... Mr. Kopperman why did you accuse your daughter of murder when you know that it is a malicious evil lie?

Jane Taylor: You said that in front of the others. Oy Vey! It's a wonder you weren't thrown out.

Rosa: They were going to.

Jane Taylor: So tell me what happened then?

Rosa: (FLASHBACK) if you do that I'll go straight to the New York Times and the Jewish Press and tell them how you caused your daughter to have a mental breakdown. I don't think the publicity would do you and this firm a lot of good.

Jane Taylor: Rosa you always seem so genteel. It's hard to imagine you as a Hatchki Brenn. So then what happened?

Rosa: He took me in to his office. We had words and soon he realised the truth and so here we are.

(CAMERA SWITCH TO DIANE, DAVE AND SAM)

Diane: I have to go to bed now. I'm feeling very tired. When will I see you again daddy?

Dave: We were just discussing that. How would you like to spend this weekend in my apartment? It's not all that far away.

Diane: Oh could I grandpa – please, please.

Sam Taylor: I don't see why not. But as you know in this home it is grandma who has the final word. Jane can you come here a moment we need a decision that only you can make.

(JANE AND ROSA COME OVER)

Jane Taylor: So what's the matter that only I can deal with?

Sam Taylor: Diane wants to spend the weekend with Dave in his apartment? Is that okay?

Jane Taylor: So why do you have to ask me if my granddaughter wants to spend time with her father? As if I would say no. What sort of a monster do you think I am?

Sam Taylor: Did I say you were a monster? All I said was –

Jane Taylor: All you said – All you said. Where was your saychell?

Sam Taylor: Diane I think your grandma means it would be nice if you and your dad were to spend some time together.

Diane: Daddy maybe you could teach me how to play chess?

Dave: (Laughs) Somehow Diane I think your grandpa would be a much better teacher. He is a very good player. I'm not in his class.

Jane Taylor: I'm sure what ever you do together it will be good.

Diane: I'm so happy – goodnight everyone –

Dave: Good night Diane (He embraces Diane and the kiss)

(FADE OUT – FADE IN TO DAVE'S CAR –
HE IS DRIVING ROSA BACK TO HER FLAT)

Dave: I'm so glad that you have brought me and my daughter together Rosa. I am eternally in your debt.

Rosa: I'm happy to have helped. Did your boss say anything after I left?

Dave: Yes – He asked me if would be visited again by that cookie woman.

Rosa: And what did you say to that?

Dave: I said I sincerely hope so.

Rosa: (laughing) what did say to that. Bet he looked puzzled.

Dave: He asked me if I was due for a vacation. I said time off would be nice but I was too busy with some new accounts. To change the subject Rosa, I wonder if you and I might see each other again. Do you like the Movies?

Rosa: I don't know I've never been.

Dave: Really – if it's not too personal a question what do you do in your spare time?

Rosa: Some of the time I prepare my lessons and up-date my reviews of each pupil and then after making and eating supper I go to bed dream about what might have been. Truth is as I told you – I cry myself to sleep.

(BY THIS TIME THEY REACH ROSA'S FLAT)

Dave: Rosa I know this my sound silly but do you think if we ever got together we could cry on each other's shoulders. And who knows maybe our ghosts would like a night off too. Maybe they might get together and talk about us. It sounds daft I know and I'm not making any sense. But I'd still like to take you out some time.

Rosa: Dave you are a very kind sweet man, who will spoil his daughter such a lot. I would like you to spoil me a little too.

Dave: (Takes Rosa's hand and kisses it) When would be the best time to call you? I can be free any time you are.

Rosa: I finish school at four I'm usually home by thirty after. I'll need to change. I can be ready for seven.

Dave: Shall we say then next Monday at seven?

Rosa: That'll be fine. There is just one thing Dave I'm still very much in love with Martin and. . . .

Dave: You mean like I still love Diana who I can never forget. I understand the position Rosa. As I said our tears will become familiar with our shoulders.

(FADE OUT – FADE IN TO JANE TAYLOR
ON THE PHONE)

Jane Taylor: To tell the truth – I'm so glad it worked out for them. You've just no idea the aggravation they had before they could marry in shul. To start with Dave wasn't all that bothered. He hardly keeps anything anyway. Not that he's a bad man at all. (Pause) That was different. When my Diana – May she rest in peace – passed away He just went to pieces. Anyway that's all in the past now. His new wife is my granddaughter's teacher. If I tell you she is such an *angel* words can't describe. The Tzorres she had with the Nazis in Germany no one should ever know of it. If that's not enough our Rabbis bless them are such Grosse Mamzayerim had to add their rules shmules. (Pause) I'm telling you it was like this (FADE OUT – FADE IN TO RABBI'S OFFICE)

Rabbi: (Looks up after reading Rosa's documents) Well everything seems in order except the death certificate.

Rosa: Rabbi I can assure you all the details are correct and –

Rabbi: Miss Smith – like you I too am a refugee from Nazi Germany and I only too well understand German – it is my mother tongue. The problem as I see it is that the Bet Din will ask for proof that Miss Smith and Rosa Deutcher are one and the same person.

Dave: I'm sorry Rabbi – this is utterly ridiculous. Rosa went through the proper United States Naturalisation procedures. Why should there be a problem?

Rabbi: The *problem* is Mr. Kopperman That this Ketuba only shows the Hebrew names of the bride and groom.

Dave: So why isn't that good enough? Rosa has a Ketuba which surely means she is Jewish and her husband was also Jewish. I don't get it.

Rabbi: Look – I'm not unsympathetic – but what can I do? How can the Bet Din be sure that this Ketuba which shows the name Leah Bas Yitzchok really belongs to Miss Rosa Smith? The Death certificate has the family name as Deutcher. Who is to say that these documents were obtained by someone desperate to leave Nazi Germany?

Dave: What do you mean *obtained* what you are suggesting is that Rosa *Stole* these papers?

Rabbi: Please – I'm only trying to point out the difficulties.

(THERE IS A KNOCK AT THE DOOR –
A MAN WALKS IN)

Man: Oh! I'm sorry Rabbi I didn't – (Notices Dave) I don't believe it; as I live and breathe Dave Kopperman. What brings you of *all* people to a Synagogue? (FADE OUT – FADE IN BACK TO JANE TAYLOR ON THE PHONE)

Jane Taylor: Well it turned out that he was an old friend of Dave's who just happened to be the Hon. Treasurer of the Shul. (Pause) I'm not sure but I heard that his wife and the Rebbitzen are not the best of friends if you get my meaning. Anyway to cut long story short; this friend of Dave's told the Rabbi straight – that if he caused any problems he and his family would join another shul. (Pause) Not quite – you see that family is full of Gvirim (Pause) they are very big in Stocks and Shares so big they own half Wall Street – really wealthy. And as we all know if you've got gelt people listen to you. (Pause) Yes – and you too keep well bye for now.

Sam Taylor: Who was that Jane?

Jane Taylor: Who do you think? My cousin Eva – can she talk – a real grosse yenta.

(FADE OUT – FADE IN TO
WEDDING RECEPTION OF DAVE AND ROSA)

Jane Taylor: Well Sam – That's it. Thank God it's all gone so well. A pity the Rabbi spoke for so long.

Sam Taylor: And about our Diane you say nothing.

Jane Taylor: What is there to say? It's clear for all to see. She looks happy and radiant – and did you notice she has had three dancing partners already?

Sam Taylor: Of course I noticed. Do think I go around with my eyes shut? I – just a second – is that Myrtle and Elmer by the window?

Jane Taylor: So who else do you know has a glass of scotch in his hand all the time at a Simcha?

Sam Taylor: Oy Gevalt he's put on some weight. Oyo he's spotted us and they are coming over. Look pleased.

Jane Taylor: Myrtle – Elmer how lovely to see you Mazal Tov! It's a long time.

Elmer: Mazal Tov! You're both looking great Kay-yen. What's the secret?

Myrtle: The secret Elmer is that Sam spends his spare time playing Chess – not drinking scotch.

Elmer: Gee Myrtle – if people don't drink at a Simcha – just when can they drink? Tell me!

Myrtle: You'd think that he never sees a bottle of scotch except at smichas.

Sam Taylor: Myrtle let me explain something to you. Your husband only drinks when he's happy. It's because you're such a devoted loving wife that he is happy all the time.

Myrtle: (Smiles knowingly) so tell me – when he is not with me like when he plays Poker with boys does he also drink?

Sam Taylor: He drinks with the boys just to be sociable. You don't seriously think he *enjoys* drinking when he plays poker?

Elmer: There you are Myrtle. You're always going on and say why can't I be more like my cousin Sam. And maybe you're right. He understands why I'm forced to drink when I play Poker.

Jane Taylor: You know Myrtle if you listen to them two long enough, you might end up believing what they say.

Sam Taylor: It's good when there is something to laugh about. There's been so much Tzores in the world and, also for the family.

Myrtle: You're so right Sam. It's such a pleasure to see your Diane looking so happy – thank God.

Elmer: Before I forget – I've invited the happy couple over to our place after the party here is over – why don't you join us as well? It'll be great talking over old times.

Myrtle: I've made him promise not to bring out his war time photographs. So you can relax.

Elmer: Listen Myrtle – some people are very interested in –

Myrtle: In enjoying themselves so *no* Photos Elmer – do you hear me?

Elmer: (Sighs) I hear you Myrtle which is why I think I should circulate some more. See you all later.

(FADE OUT – FADE IN TO ELEMER AND MYRTLE'S APARTMENT. ELMER, SAM AND DAVE ARE IN A GROUP TALKING ABOUT THE ECONOMY AND POLITICS. MYRTLE, JANE AND ROSA ARE IN A GROUP TALKING ABOUT CLOTHES AND MEN)

Myrtle: That's what has always puzzled me about men. They've just no idea what to buy – even for themselves. If I didn't go with Elmer to buy his suits – you can't imagine what he'd come home with. And as for costume jewellery for me – well I've always got to take it back to the store. I just don't understand it.

Jane Taylor: Myrtle – what can you expect? All they know is football and baseball. Where would they get the time to think as well? It's a miracle the know how to make a living. Am I not right Rosa?

Rosa: I believe it was an American song writer who wrote 'A good man is hard to find' (They all laugh)

Elmer: (In a loud voice) Myrtle I hope you were not laughing at us.

Myrtle: Of course not my hero – I was just saying how good you are at choosing the right clothes and that you taste in jewellery is perfect. (More laughter from the ladies)

Elmer: How about some coffee. Who's for coffee anyone or maybe something a little stronger?

Myrtle: *Elmer* we will *all* have coffee. You make it so well. Off you go.

(FADE OUT – FADE IN TO ELMER SERVING COFFEE
OFFERS THE TRAY TO ROSA – HE NOTICES THE
BROOCH IN THE LAPEL OF HER JACKET.)

Elmer: That's an unusual brooch Rosa – and yet I could swear
I've seen one similar – have you had it long.

Rosa: It was given to me many years ago. Are you interested in
jewellery?

Elmer: No – not particularly – but I'm sure I've –

Myrtle: Elmer leave the bride alone. The rest of us may not be as
pretty as she is but we are waiting for our coffee.

Elmer: Here you are folks – I was just interested in –

Myrtle: We *know* what you were interested in just – *Elmer* there
is no sugar, there is no cream, *how* can I drink my coffee?

Elmer: I'm sorry Myrtle – I'll go and get some. I know I've seen
a brooch like Rosa's somewhere. It'll bug me till remember. (Gets
up and goes to the kitchen)

Myrtle: You must excuse him Rosa. He sees a pretty woman
and he'll do anything – make up any excuse to engage her in
conversation.

Dave: That's okay Myrtle – Rosa has me to protect her.

Elmer: (Enters with tray of sugar and cream) Sugar and cream as
you requested my love.

Myrtle: Don't you *my love* me. You Casanova.

Elmer: Oh come on Myrtle – what's with the Casanova business?
All I said was my love. What's wrong with that?

Myrtle: You know perfectly well what I mean. Every time I catch you flirting with another woman you call me my love to hide your guilt.

Elmer: (Looks around at the company) so what did I do wrong? I remarked to Rosa that her unusual Brooch seemed familiar. For that she calls me Casanova.

Sam Taylor: Enough already you too. You're giving me a headache.

Jane Taylor: Now Sam – if Elmer and myrtle wish to .....to .....

Sam Taylor: To what? Tell me what? Have an argument. I'm sorry I don't need to hear it. It takes me all my health and strength when *you* decide to argue with me. I don't have to leave my home to listen to another poor husband get it in the neck. What do you think I'm some sort of a Masochist?

Jane Taylor: Why don't you just drink your coffee and then explain why you and Elmer have not volunteered to go help out in Israel?

Sam Taylor: Listen lady – if I were just twenty years younger I'd be there right on the front line. What do you say Elmer?

Elmer: I haven't told anyone but I *have* volunteered.

Sam Taylor: So how come you're still here?

Elmer: Well it's like this. When I told them I drove a tank during the war they asked if they could put me on stand-by. So naturally I said yes.

Myrtle: You never told me Elmer. When did all this happen and why wasn't I informed. I am your *wife* just in case you have forgotten.

Elmer: Gee Myrtle come on when do I get a chance to tell you anything? The only chance I get to speak in this house is when I am answering your questions.

Dave: Well folks it's time Rosa and I were off. We've both got busy weeks ahead.

Myrtle: So how come you're not going on Honeymoon?

Rosa: Today was the only time we could have the chuppa and we both are tied up at work till next week. *Then* Dave is taking me to meet his relatives in Philadelphia.

Myrtle: Rosa let me wish you both Mazal Tov once again and let's get together again soon.

All to Dave &Rosa: Good Night and Mazal Tov.

(FADE OUT – FADE IN TO MYRTLE AND ELEMER'S
BEDROOM – MYRTLE IN BED WANTING TO
PUT THE LIGHTS OFF AND GO TO SLEEP.
ELMER HAS A PILE OF PHOTOGRAPHS
IN HIS HAND AND IS SCRUTINISING THEM)

Myrtle: Elmer what are you doing? Come to bed already it's late.

Elmer: Just a little while longer. I *think* I know where I've seen that brooch Rosa ---

Myrtle: Vita mit der brooch! As I leave and breath I am sure when they put me in my coffin the last words I'll hear on this earth will be *I'm sure I've seen that brooch before.* Elmer come to bed now – enough already.

Elmer: Okay! Okay! Just a – aha I *knew* I'd seen that brooch before. Myrtle just take a look a this photo.

Myrtle: (Exasperated – takes the photo – sits up in bed) Elmer what are you hacking me on a chynik about a brooch? All I see is four soldiers – aha I recognise you. So show me where the brooch is then let's go to sleep.

Elmer: You see the guy standing next to me – look closely at his left lapel. What do you see?

Myrtle: (Looks carefully – a longish pause) There's something pinned there. Can't say what it is though. Besides it's a black and white photo and it's too small to say what it is .*Now* Elmer can we go to sleep?

Elmer: (Climbs into bed – switches off the lights) you know what I'm going to do Myrtle?

Myrtle: Please God you're going to sleep – but somehow I get the feeling you're not.

Elmer: I'm so sure that the guy next to me in that photograph was wearing the identical brooch to –

Myrtle: (In a loud but drowsy voice) Gott in Himmel? What does this meshuggena husband of mine want of my life and that brooch? Just say what you're going to do – then not another word – do you hear me Elmer – not another word.

Elmer: I was just going to say that in the morning I'll take the photo to be enlarged and that –

Myrtle: Wonderful! I'm so pleased. Good *night Elmer.*

(FADE OUT – FADE IN TO DAVE AND ROSA'S APARTMENT. IT IS ABOUT 7.00 P.M. AND THEY ARE HAVING SUPPER. THE PHONE RINGS)

Dave: I'll get it (gets up. walks towards the phone) Oh by the way did I mention that I'd like Diane to come with us next week?

Rosa: Yes you told *me* did you say anything to Jane and Sam?

Dave: (Lifts receiver) Hello – just a moment please hold the line. No I forgot. I'll phone them. Hello Dave Kopperman here. Hello Elmer nice to hear from you how's things?

Elmer: Fine thanks – are you and your lovely wife well?

Dave: We're well thanks. To what do we owe the pleasure of this call?

Elmer: You know when you and Rosa were at our place and I mentioned that I'd seen a brooch like the one Rosa was wearing. Well I now know where I'd seen it.

Dave: Oh *really*? How did you come by this? (Put his hand over the mouthpiece and calls out to Rosa) It's Elmer he's talking about your brooch. So say that again Elmer – you have a wartime photo of you and a guy wearing a similar brooch. (Pauses) Let me check with Rosa – we are still quite busy preparing for our trip to Philadelphia next week. (Puts hand over mouthpiece) He wants to come over and show us the photograph. I think a *long story* is also part of the visit. What do you think? Shall I put him off?

Rosa: Ask him if Myrtle would like to come too?

Dave: Rosa says she'd like to see Myrtle again. (Pause) Oh I see you don't think Myrtle is keen to talk about the brooch. (Pause) Tomorrow night say about six and then you could go straight off to your Poker game. Where's it being held? (Short pause) That's not far from us. So even if you made for a half after six you'd still make it in good time. (Longish pause) and you look forward to it – bye.

(FADE OUT – FADE IN TO DAVE AND ROSA'S FLAT.
IT'S JUST AFTER 06.30 THE DOOR BELL RINGS)

Dave: Okay I'll get it. (Opens door) Hi Elmer nice to see you come in – fancy a coffee. Rosa will join us shortly. So how are things with you and Myrtle?

Elmer: Same as always. She complains. I plead guilty. And so it goes on.

Dave: I'm sure it can't be all that bad. Let's face it you'd be lost without her.

Elmer: Maybe – you could be – Oh hello Rosa how nice to see you.

Rosa: And it's good to see you – can I get you a coffee or something?

Elmer: Thanks but no. I daren't be late for Poker. The guys would lynch me. I just wanted to show you this photo. (He passes it to Dave) it's an enlargement I had done early today. It was taken a few months before the end of the war. It was in a place called Bad Harzberg. Can you recognise me? I've put on one or two pounds since then. Well the standing next to me he is wearing a brooch just like Rosa's but it curves the other way.

Dave: It does look very much like it. But it's not easy to tell from a black and white film. Here Rosa – take a look.

Rosa: (Takes the photo and turns pale) I – I – don't understand – when did you say. . . . (Voices trails off and she starts to shake)

Dave: Rosa! What's the matter?

Rosa: I – I don't feel very well please excuse me.

Dave: (Suddenly remembers – Flash Back – you see Dave that is all I have of my Marriage – a Ketuba a Death certificate and a brooch . . . Elmer would you mind very much if kept the photo – I can't explain.

Elmer: Sure Dave that's why I brought it. I thought you might find it interesting. Is Rosa going to be all right – she looked very pale. Anyway I must be off – hope Rosa soon feels better. I'll see myself out. Good night.

Dave: Good night Elmer – regards to Myrtle. (Goes into the bedroom) Rosa you don't look well at all. Do you think I should call a Doctor?

Rosa: Oh Dave – I'm so confused. Elmer's photo. It makes no sense.

Dave: (Sits beside her and puts and arm around her shoulders) the guy in the photo wearing the brooch – you think it was your husband. I'm right aren't I?

Rosa: (Embraces Dave) Hold me tight! I just don't understand how it could be. Why was I given a Death certificate in 1939? Why hasn't Martin tried to contact me? And what about us? Where does it leave us? Can we? - -

Dave: The first thing we must do is try to calm down. (Kisses her) the next thing is to try and trace Martin: or at least find out what happened to him.

Rosa: Yes Dave – but where *does* that leave us? I was just beginning to find happiness and –

Dave: And we *will* remain happy. Tell you what – if you are up to it we'll take another look at the photo. Can you be 100% sure that it *is* Martin. You don't think it might be someone who *looks* like him. And the brooch – there must be others just like yours. Maybe it's just coincidences?

Rosa: Dave you must be the kindest man in the world. Know what I envy the three years you and Diana had together. We've been married now for just a few days and already I'm making you unhappy.

Dave: You mustn't say that Rosa. I'll pretend you never said that. The thing is to get the matter sorted. We can't do anything tonight. Tell you what – let's set the alarm for six. After a night's sleep we'll think clearer. Agreed?

Rosa: (Whispers) Agreed.

(FADE OUT – FADE IN TO THE FOLLOWING MORNING. DAVE AND ROSA ARE DRINKING COFFEE AND EATING TOAST. THE PHOTO IS ON THE TABLE)

Dave: So – you *are* positive it is Martin. I know this may sound silly – but by any chance did he have a twin brother?

Rosa: (Smiles) I don't know – I only met his half brother Hans. I never asked him about anyone else. We hardly had time to talk about things. Everything was done in a whirl.

Dave: We need to know more from Elmer about the photo.

Rosa: Yes – the exact date it was taken would help a lot.

Dave: Shall I phone the school and tell them you are sick and won't be in today?

Rosa: No – I'll feel better doing something.

Dave: You are sure now. I wouldn't want –

Rosa: I'm sure Dave – really.

(FADE OUT – FADE IN TO THE EVENING. DAVE AND ROSA ARE HAVING SUPPER)

Rosa: So were you able to contact Elmer.

Dave: I'll say. Do you know I couldn't stop him talking. Must have been at least an hour on the phone. Myrtle was out for the day so I suppose he took the opportunity to talk.

Rosa: Did he have any more information about the photo?

Dave: You bet he did! Seems the guy with the brooch was attached to Elmer's Tank core. He was an Acting Master Sergeant sent by the British. He spoke good English but with a German – or some sort of European accent. His job was to identify – White Rose Society members and –

Rosa: (Drops her glass of fruit juice) There's no doubt it *was* Martin. He could still be alive. Did Elmer say what the man's name was?

Dave: (Looks anxious) the guys called him Marty. Are you okay Rosa?

Rosa: Yes – with you saying the White Rose Society that –

Dave: I don't understand – who was the White –

Rosa: Germans who actively opposed the Nazis. Did you manage to find out anything else?

Dave: When I eventually finished talking to Elmer – or should I say *listening* to him I got on to the British Embassy in Washington. The upshot was they gave me an address to write to at the Embassy.

Rosa: Do you think it will help?

Dave: What they actually said was – put into writing what I'd asked for and that I'd receive a reply within a month. They said they couldn't discuss the matter further over the phone.

Rosa: (Excitedly) so it looks as if they know something.

Dave: I wouldn't raise your hopes *too* high. But as you say - they must know something.

(FADE OUT – FADE IN TO DAVE AND ROSA'S FLAT – IT IS ONE MONTH LATER. THEY ARE HAVING BREAKFAST. THE DOORBELL RINGS)

Dave: Who can that be at this time?

Rosa: I'm enjoying this piece of toast – so I think *you* should answer the door.

Dave: (gets up and goes to the door) Morning Mr.Mailman.

Mailman: Sign here please.

Dave: Okay – that's it – thank you – have a nice day. (Closes the door) There's one for you – from the Art Gallery in Philadelphia. We certainly had a terrific vacation. Diane was excited all the time and you seemed a lot happier. And – this is for me from the British Embassy. Shall I read it – or would you prefer to read it in private?

Rosa: (Voice trembling) I think you'd better read it. I don't –

Dave: Okay Rosa – try stay calm. Whatever it says – I'm here for you.

Rosa: (A little impatient) Oh *do* get *on* with it.

Dave: (opens letter) Right – here goes 'Dear Mr. Kopperman Thank you for – Blah! Blah! Blah! The person in question was involved in certain activities for the Allies – the nature of which is classified. I am permitted to tell you that he was a member of a unit know as Group 69. This involved operations in Occupied Germany during WW2 and for sometime after. A number of them were in East Germany after WW2. There has been no communication with them since that time and there whereabouts are unknown. We have contacted the East German Government through a number of diplomatic channels, giving a list of names. A few days ago we were notified that none of the named personnel

– including the subject of your enquiry – were in East Germany. They would not confirm or deny whether or not they had ever been in that country. Yours Sincerely etc. etc. etc.

Rosa: I don't know what to make of that. I'm more confused than ever.

Dave: It seems to me that they are saying that it *is* Martin in the photo. He must have been involved with Military Intelligence. Did you know which city in Germany he came from?

Rosa: He came from Stuttgart but he spent many years in Leipzig.

Dave: Leipzig – which is in East Germany – so his local Knowledge could have been of use to the Allies. In fact he *could still* be there which is why they don't mention him by name in the letter.

Rosa: So where does that leave us Dave? How I wish I'd never seen that photo. (Breaks down crying)

Dave: (Embraces her and kisses her) Rosa I'm going to say something now that you may not like. So promise you'll not be angry with me?

Rosa: (Startled) Angry with you Dave. You may never be able to replace my Knight in shining armour – but you are the kindest man I've known or would ever want to know. (Sobbing slows down)

Dave: You make me sound much better than I really am Rosa. Nice though it is to hear your words. Well it's like this. The way I see it is –all our trouble started with Elmer's photograph. So like you said you wish you'd never seen it. So lets forget we ever saw it and drop the matter altogether. What do you think? You don't have to answer now. Think about it and we'll talk about it after work. Agreed?

Rosa: Agreed – You know Dave – if only I could have met you first.

(FADE OUT – FADE IN TO DAVE AND
ROSA'S FLAT THAT EVENING)

Dave: (Opening entrance door) Hi Rosa – what's to eat? I'm starved.

Rosa: How does cheese omelette sound?

Dave: Great! I fancy a beer – do you want anything from the fridge?

Rosa: If we still have any orange juice – I'll have some.

Dave: You're in luck. (Lowers voice) Have you had any thoughts about what we were talking about this morning?

Rosa: I was all for it before lunch. Then during lunch hour I called at the Doctor's Surgery.

Dave: Why what's wrong?

Rosa: I've been feeling queasy and a little dizzy lately so I thought I go for a check up.

Dave: Did they give you anything for it? Did they say what it was?

Rosa: They couldn't give me anything because I'm not ill. It looks as though Diane will be a sister in the fall.

Dave: Diane! I don't understand – you went – (Hits his forehead with his hand) you mean you are – are?

Rosa: (Laughs) Oh Dave I wish you could see your face. It's the best tonic I've had in weeks. Yes I am pregnant.

Dave: (After a brief pause) I know I should be overjoyed.

Rosa: I think I know why you are not. You're *not* pleased are you Dave?

Dave: I'm both pleased and not pleased. I know it sounds stupid. But the last time my wife was pregnant it lead to her death and now we're not certain whether your Martin is alive. And if he is can we still be legally married. And the status of *our* unborn child. It's just too much.

Rosa: You know Dave I love you more now. Even more than before.

Dave: Wow! That's great for me. But do mind telling me why?

Rosa: Because my sweet kind Dave you showed concern for *our* unborn child. You could have said *your* unborn child.

Dave: (Sniffles and wipes away a tear) I suppose it still boils down to whether or not we ignore that damn photograph.

Rosa: (Entwines her arms around his neck and kisses him and in a soft voice) photograph! What photograph?

(FADE OUT) (IT IS NOW 1969. DAVE AND ROSA'S DAUGHTER IS TWENTY AND WANTS TO MARRY. DIANE IS 34 AND IS MARRIED WITH TWO CHILDREN. MARTIN DEUTCHER – NOW KNOWN AS MARTIN SMYTH IS IN HIS OFFICE IN PHILEDELPHIA. THE PHONE RINGS)

Martin: Yes who is it?

Receptionist: It's a Mr. Ted Dane from a firm in Chicago called Engineering Optics. He wants to arrange a meeting. Is that okay?

Martin: Yes sure – but I'm busy all this week. Next week will be fine.

Receptionist: Very good sir.

Martin: (About to go to filing cabinet when the phone rings) Yes Joan who is it now?

Receptionist: It's Doc James – you wanted to talk to him.

Martin: (exasperated) okay Joan put him through – and Joan please no more calls today – just take messages okay?

Receptionist: Very well Mr. Smyth.

Martin: Hello Doc. Good to hear from you. Yes as we arranged – my place at eight sharp. (Pause) You know what they say Doc. Old habits die hard. It goes back to my childhood in Germany. (Pause) sure bring him along too. (Pause) No I am the cook. That's the advantage of being single – you have to learn many skills. In fact though I say it myself I'm pretty good at it. Tell you what we'll let your charming wife adjudicate. (Intercom buzzes) Just a second Doc. Please hold I have a call on the other line. Joan I said no more calls – what is it now?

Receptionist: Sorry Mr. Smyth, the Rep. who phoned earlier Ted. Dane from Engineering Optics is here. He just wants to leave his card and Catalogue.

Martin: Okay – bring it in to me – and get rid of him I'm very busy. And please Joan – definitely no more calls.

Receptionist: Very good sir.

Martin: Hi Doc. Sorry about that – the demands of business.

(Receptionist enters Martins office and places catalogue and card in front of Martin)

Martin: (Makes a cursory glance at the business card) by the way I take it that you – (Stops speaking and takes a closer look at the card – he gasps) Doc. I'll call you back something urgent has just cropped up – bye. (Dashes into Reception) Joan has that Rep gone?

Receptionist: Just a moment ago. I let use the washroom before–

Martin: Go get him back -!

Receptionist: Sir? I –

Martin: Now Joan *Now* I must speak to him. Gone on move Schnell *schnell.*

Receptionist: Okay sir I'm going – I'm going! (Dashes out)

(FADE OUT – FADE IN TO MARTIN'S OFFICE – DOOR OPENS)

Receptionist: Mr. Dane Sir

Martin: Thank you Joan. Come in Mr. Dane please take a seat.

Mr. Dane: Thanks for your time Mr.Smyth. Your Secretary said it was urgent.

Martin: Just a moment Mr. Dane (Buzzes Intercom) Joan absolutely no more calls – oh and Joan – sorry If I sounded sharp just before. Tell you what if you can bring today's work up to date you can have the day off tomorrow. Right Mr. Dane your card reads Agents for Zimmerschaft products.

Mr. Dane: Yes indeed we handle all their products. Is there any in particular that interests you?

Martin: What I want to know is who is in charge of Zimmerschaft and where are they based?

Mr. Dane: Like us they are based in Chicago and the main man is Mr. Hans Zimmerschaft – but I should point out –

Martin: Never mind that – do you have a contact number for him?

Mr. Dane: (searches in his wallet) I have the number for their Admin. Office

Martin: Please let me have it.

Mr. Dane: Sure – here it is.

Martin: (Presses intercom) Joan please come here a moment.

Receptionist: On my way sir – (Enters office)

Martin: Get me this number and when you are through say you have a very urgent call for Mr.Zimmerschaft from Mr. Martin Deutcher. Got that?

Receptionist: Y – Yes – you did say Martin Deutcher? (Looks around puzzled)

Martin: Joan – just do as I ask. Then put the call through to me. Understood?

Receptionist: Very good sir. I'm on to it right now (exits office)

Mr. Dane: I wonder if these light weight binoculars would be a good seller for you Mr.Smyth. It has a connection for super focus operated by the Zimmerschaft auto mechanism. It come with case and with the attachment is only $149.99 dollars. Without the attachment only – (Intercom buzzes)

Receptionist: I have Mr.Zimmerschafts Secretary on line two.

Martin: Put her through – Hello (Pause) Yes that's right (Pauses) Then I must ask you to interrupt the meeting and tell Mr.Zimmerschaft that his *brother Martin* wants to speak to him. Yes I said his brother. Okay I'll hold. (Turns his attention to Mr. Dane) Look make an appointment with my receptionist for next

Tuesday – and be sure to bring a sample of those binoculars you mentioned – Okay – goodbye. (Pause) Yes Hans it's me Martin – it's great just know you're alive and well. Can we arrange to meet soon?

(FADE OUT – FADE IN TO HANS HOUSE. IT IS
THE SATURDAY AFTER THEIR PHOCE
CONVERSATION. THEY ARE EATING LUNCH)

Hans: You have put on quite a bit of weight over the years Martin. To what do you owe it to?

Martin: Unlike you Hans – I don't have a wife to watch over me. I do my own cooking or dine out. Where is your wife by the way I was hoping to meet her?

Hans: She was called away this morning. Urgent legal problem.

Martin: I don't suppose by any chance you have any idea what happened to Rosa.

Hans: I knew you were bound to ask me that. I think we'd better go into the other room. I've quite a selection of scotch to choose from. (They leave the table and go into the lounge) What would you prefer?

Martin: I'm a Jack Daniels man – if you have?

Hans: I have (Pours out a treble) here.

Martin: Thanks – a very generous portion if you don't mind me saying so.

Hans: You'll need it my dear brother after hearing what I have to tell you. (Raises his glass) Here's to family understanding.

Martin: I'll drink to that. So tell me Hans what *did* happen to you and Rosa?

Hans: We were making our way to the Swiss border. There were traffic diversions all over. In short we ended up In Celle under arrest. I was forced to give Rosa a copy of *your* Death certificate.

Martin: *Death certificate?* What are you talking about? How - -

Hans: Let me explain (FLASH BACK) . . . . . please Rosa – I know you are shocked – the truth is Headquarters dictated the details over the phone to the Superintendent which is why he must countersign................. Greta can you hide Rosa in Your truck. And that was the last I saw of Rosa. I never had chance to explain.

Martin: But surely when you were in the shelter you could have–

Hans: There just wasn't time. There were so many people about. Remember in those you couldn't trust anybody. Who knows who might have overheard? And besides we'd only just got in when my cousin Greta spotted me.

Martin: (Gulps his whiskey) have you tried to locate your cousin.

Hans: I tried but unfortunately she was killed during an air-raid. Did you ever think of advertising in Missing Persons for Rosa?

Martin: Couldn't.

Hans: Why ever not.

Martin: I can't explain fully other than to say that because of what I did for the Allies during the war my Identity – that is my *true* identity must remain a secret.

Hans: Is that why you never re-married? Because you don't know where Rosa (Voice trails off)

Martin: There is that – but the truth is I'm still very much in love with Rosa. I just can't get her out of my mind. Could I have another whiskey?

Hans: Sure. I'll have another as well. So what now Martin?

Martin: (Gulps at his whiskey) I'll just carry on with my business and let the future take care of itself. And you Hans have you any family?

Hans: Did have. We had a son who had lots of ambition but was headstrong and no business acumen. He was conned in to parting with his money. Ended up with large debts he couldn't meet. So he took his own life. My wife still cries for him.

Martin: Oh Hans – I'm so sorry. What happened to the Con Artist? Do you know him?

Hans: Oh yes I *know* him alright and between you and me I will have my revenge. Make no mistake about it.

Martin: You are not planning to (Voice trails off)

Hans: Oh good heavens no. One thing I learned in the Gestapo was to be thorough and meticulous. Believe you me I know how to bide my time. Very soon he plans to marry and that could provide the opportunity I've been waiting for.

Martin: So just how are you keeping tabs on him.

Hans: I have a detective agency that gives me a weekly report.

Martin: That must be very expensive Hans.

Hans: It is – but that's not important. I've also two of my own employees tailing him. In fact I know he will be getting married in your city.

Martin: In Philadelphia? Tell you what give me his name and I'll join your intelligence team.

(THEY BOTH GULP THEIR WHISKIES –
AND HANS POURS MORE)

Hans: What can I say?

Martin: Don't say anything – just bear in mind anyone who attacks *my* family attacks me. Make no mistake Hans we'll get him.

Hans: Let's drink to that. Cheers

Martin: Cheers. What's the crooks name?

Hans: Phil Nirobbman

Martin: He'll be sorry he started with my brother. Hans I must go catch my plane. Best regards to your Wife. Hope to see you both soon.

(FADE OUT – FADE IN TO ART GALLERY IN PHILEDELPHIA. THERE IS AN EXIBITION ABOUT JEWISH ART. MARTIN IS THERE. SO IS ROSA'S DAUGHTER JANET AND DIANE IS THERE WITH HER TWO YOUNG CHILDREN AS WELL AS A PRIVATE DETECTIVE WORKING FOR HANS.)

Martin: I'm not so keen on this abstract stuff. Why is this one included anyway in an exhibition of *Jewish* art? What's the *Jewish* element? To me all abstract so called art is the same.

Guide: This painting is the creation of a Jewish artist sir. She was a refugee from Nazi Germany. (Address the rest of the group) This gentleman says he cannot identify anything particularly Jewish about this painting. Can any of you provide him with an answer?

Diane: Yes I can. (She steps forward and speaks to Martin) The artist is my Aunt Rosa – at least I call her my aunt because she married my father. I was one of her pupils.

Martin: So you know how the artist thinks. So where is her *Jewish* theme in this painting?

Diane: You see all the dark colours represent sadness and the bright ones happiness. Where they intermingle they ---

Diane's daughter: Mommy! Mommy! Can we go now I'm tired and want –

Diane: Phyllis – don't be rude. I'm talking to the gentleman. You will forgive her she's usually so good and –

Phyllis: Mommy – the man is wearing a brooch just like grandmas

Diane: *Phyllis* why are you being so ---

Martin: That's okay – did you say your aunt is called *Rosa* a German Refugee and she has a brooch like this?

Diane: Yes Mr.?

Martin: Smyth – with a Y – do you have a contact number for your aunt? I'm interested in jewellery especially brooches like this.

Diane: It could be difficult – you see she lives in New York and she could be on the way here. Her daughter – my half sister is getting married this Sunday and there is such a lot to do. Why not have a word *with* my sister – she's over there by the landscape paintings. Better still I'll take you over and introduce you.

(FADE OUT – FADE IN TO BAR IN PHILADEPHIA.
HANS PRIVATE EYE APPROACHES JOAN,
MARTINS RECEPTIONIST)

Private Eye: Hey gorgeous you look like a lady who appreciates good company *and* even better a drink. What will you have?

Joan: I'd like a nice quiet evening to relax. I'm not in a chatty mood.

Private Eye: That's fine lady. You listen while I talk. Barman – Scotch on the rocks and my friend here will have?

Joan: Make mine an Angel's kiss. So tell me what's so important that you have to talk about.

Private Eye: You know that big Jewish wedding scheduled for Sunday?

Joan: Sure who doesn't? The Koppermans and the Nirobbmans. It's all over the inside pages.

Private Eye: Well in a short while I'm going to make a phone call that will ruin the whole affair.

Joan: Are you saying that *just* to impress me?

Private Eye: If you *are* impressed that is one welcome added bonus. The fact is though I'm being truthful and serious.

Joan: My my that is a first. A guy in a bar not telling lies I *am* impressed. So what's the big deal?

Private Eye: I don't suppose you heard of a company called Zimmerschaft Products.

Joan: (Hesitates – she decides to lie) Means nothing to me

Private Eye: Well the big boss hates the Bridegroom.

Joan: Why? What for?

Private Eye: That – as they say in the Novels – is *another* story. The thing is I have found out that the Bride's mother is a Bigamist.

Joan: So why should that have anything to do with the Bridegroom?

Private Eye: It's to with Jewish religious law. It means that the Bride is a bastard and cannot marry someone who is legit.

Joan: How do you know all this?

Private Eye: It's my job to find things out. I'm an Enquiry Agent.

Joan: I can't work out how you know all this. What gave you a clue?

Private Eye: To cut a long story short; I've been tailing the Koppermans and yesterday they were in the Art Gallery when they get talking to this guy who was wearing a diamond brooch in his Jacket lapel. Anyway I remembered having a chat with the boss of Zimmerschaft who told me about his brother and his brother's wife who gave each other brooches. Just like the guy I saw in the Art Gallery. Which means - -

Joan: (Looks at watch and gasps) – Oh my is that the time? Must dash nice talking to you. We should do it again sometime. Bye (Hurries out)

(FADE OUT – FADE IN TO JOAN'S FLAT. SHE IS ON THE PHONE TO MARTIN . . . . .)

Joan: Forgive me for calling you at home something to tell you. But. .

(FADE OUT – FADE IN). . . Like the guy I saw in the gallery.

Martin: Thank you for calling me Joan. You did the right thing. I'll not be in the office tomorrow. So you are in charge. If anyone asks for me just say I was called away on family business and you've no idea when I'll be back.

Joan: Very good Mr.Smyth. Good night.

Martin: Good night Joan – and thanks again. (Replaces receiver – and picks it up. Dials another number) I need to speak urgently to Mrs. Rosa Kopperman. Is she available? (A short pause)

Rosa: Rosa Kopperman speaking – who is that?

Martin: They call me Mr. Smyth among other things. I need to speak to you – but not over the phone. I know your Daughter is due to be married on Sunday and what I have to say could affect things. Can you be at Cafe Ramon at two tomorrow afternoon? It really is very urgent.

Rosa: I really don't think I can. I'm so busy with the wedding and everything. In what way could my daughter's wedding be affected?

Martin: It's a very delicate matter Mrs. Kopperman – how can I put this? (Pause) I *am* right in thinking you were married before in Germany. That is correct isn't it?

Rosa: (Gasps) how did you know that? Just tell me what it is you want?

Martin: I want your daughter to have a happy marriage.

Rosa: Mr. Smyth you are confusing and upsetting me please state your business or hang up.

Martin: All I can say over the phone is someone you know in Chicago is an enemy of the Bridegroom. Please say you will meet me it really is important.

Rosa: Mr.Smyth you are confusing me even more so. Just who is this *enemy* in Chicago?

Martin: Does the name Hans Zimmerschaft mean anything to you? I'm sure it does.

Rosa: Hans is *alive* and in Chicago.

Martin: Yes – I can only explain further if you'll meet me. It is urgent and what I have to tell you won't take long.

Rosa: Very well. Tomorrow at two Cafe Ramon.

Martin: Thank you Mrs. Kopperman – It is very important. Till tomorrow then goodbye.

(FADE OUT – FADE IN – MARTIN IS PHONING
THE CAFE RAMON)

Martin: Yes that's it exactly. When she is seated bring the black coffee and a black forest gateau and the musicians must play the Blue Danube Waltz.

(FADE OUT – FADE IN - ROSA ENTERS THE CAFE –
A WAITER APPROACHES)

Rosa: I'm supposed to meet a Mr Smyth here at two I am a little early.

Waiter: You are Mrs. Kopperman I take it.

Rosa: Yes that's right.

Waiter: Please follow me Madam. There is a table booked for you. Mr.Smyth sends his apologies he will be just a few minuets late.

(Rosa sits down and the Piano and string trio play the Blue Danube Waltz as the waiter brings coffee and some black forest gateaus.)

Rosa: I didn't order ---

Martin (Gets up from an adjacent table) that's right Rosa *you* didn't order – *I* did. (He removes his dark glasses and sits opposite Rosa)

Rosa: Oh no! Say it's not true! It can't be you Martin I have a death certificate even though I saw your photo . . .

Martin: (Removes brooch from lapel and puts it on the table) It is me Rosa and I've longed for you every day and night since we parted.

Rosa: But this ruins everything. My husband, my daughter the wedding. (Breaks down crying.)

Martin: Mine gelipte sherne Rosa – I know my presence can cause trouble which is why I have decide to take certain steps to help you and your daughter who might have been *my* daughter also- in another world at another time.

Rosa: Martin – *Martin* I never stopped loving you even after I – even after I had your death certificate. Why was I made to think you were dead? Why did Hans? ---

Martin: Rosa mine dear gelipte – listen while there is still time. I met Hans in Chicago last week. (FLASHBACK) What's the Crooks name? Philip Nirobbman. . . .

Rosa: So how do you think Hans will have his revenge?

Martin: The Detective Agency that Hans used has many Jewish agents. I know that one of them has advised Hans to contact the Rabbis because your daughter has the status of Mamzer she can only marry another Mamzer.

Rosa: Yet again the Jewish religion has brought me unhappiness. Oh how I hate being Jewish. My Father ran off when I was a child and sends my mother a Get leaving his children abandoned. Then Hitler deprives us of our lives and rights. And now once again – more trouble. And another thing – *you* never made any effort to find me all these years not even an advert in the press or –

Martin: There was no way I could have done that Rosa. You see when I eventually made it to England I was sent to a Detention camp in a place called the Isle of Man. It's a small island off the

North west coast of England. When they eventually realised I was not a Nazi spy – their Military Intelligence needed German speaking interrogators. Even now I cannot use my original name. You may have heard that in Britain they have an Official Secrets Act and I am still bound by it.

Rosa: But what about my Daughter Janet – and this Mamzer problem?

Martin: I have a solution Rosa. The problem is that Rosa Kopperman was married to a Herr Martin Deutcher. You have a death certificate from the Gestapo and countersigned by a German Police Superintendent. So officially Martin Deutcher is dead. There are only *two* people in the world who know that at this moment he is still alive; you and Hans. It would be better if for you and your family if I were to die again.

Rosa: Martin – what are you saying – you must not do anything silly.

Martin: Silly you say – oh no Rosa not silly – drastic – maybe but silly?

Rosa: Martin I'm not sure what you are up to – but I don't like it. You came into my life all those years ago. You made me *so so* happy then hours later you disappeared leaving me broken and unhappy. And here you are again bringing me more sorrow. What sort of evil spirit makes you so keen to fill my life with guilt and misery? You are cruel – and god help me I *still* love you.

Martin: (Takes her hand) Rosa toward the end of the war I was attached to an American army Tank unit, in occupied Germany. It was my duty to identify as many members of the White Rose Society as possible and see that they were protected. It was a dangerous job and if we had been caught by the Nazi – well you can imagine what would have happened. So I was given (He puts his hand in a pocket and withdraws a glass phial) these are Cyanide pills. One pill is enough.

Rosa: No Martin you mustn't – there has to be another way.

Martin: Rosa – this time the death certificate will show the name Martin Smyth – with a Y. Officially Martin Deutcher is already dead. The Gestapo were always meticulous. Goodbye Rosa – it will only take seconds – Just remember I die for your love and your daughter's happiness (Opens the phial – pours the contents down his throat – reaches for his coffee, Raises the cup to his lips. Falls backwards in his chair.

Rosa: (Stands up – screams and reaches across to Martin. The table falls over.

(FLASHBACK)

Chess Player: I'm pleased you appreciate my beautiful combination. A double pawn on my queen's file and both my knights attacking the eighth rank.

(Ironic cheers and applause as well as the sobbing of Rosa)

THE END

(Copyright – Asher Drapkin – 23 Mar. 05)

'The Magic Glass'
by Asher Drapkin

Jake and his grandfather were on an outing to a castle It was the castle on which the ornament in grandfather's house was modelled. It was situated about ten miles from Jake's home, on top of a steep hill. Although mostly ruins, one wall and a tower were still intact. After they had reached the top of the tower, Grandfather said, "There are lots of legends about this castle Jake. Let me tell you about Dennis, Gwenyth and the magic glass . . . .

Gwyneth was upset. Why wouldn't her parents listen to her? Okay – so what if her father was a Physics Professor and her mother a Maths teacher. Gwyneth knew more than what they did. Everyone knew that Gwenyth was a mathematical genius, but because she was only thirteen years old, all the adults tried to prove they were cleverer than her.

Well the truth was they were not. And if that were not bad enough, she had no friends of her own age. Other children were either jealous of her – or Gwenyth thought most of them were stupid. To-day however Gwyneth was more upset than usual. Her father had designed and made a prototype Time-Machine, and was about to commence his first experiment. There was a fault in the design – or so Gwenyth thought. She tried to explain to her father what the fault was, but, like all the adults he knew better than a thirteen year old girl. As for her mother – well Maths teacher she may be. But she had no idea about 'Gyroscopic Terrestrial Fixed Torque Differentials.' Gwyneth however did know.

So she prepared herself for the TIME journey. She went down into the basement study and gathered her father's favourite armchair, magnifying glass, binoculars, telescope and her favourite book entitled 'Tales of Wizards and Witches' and placed them exactly in the centre of the study. She sat in the chair and waited. It was not long before her journey began.

Her father was in his laboratory-cum-workshop that was situated directly above the basement studio. He adjusted the Time machine controls and began the experiment by pressing the 'Start' button. Nothing happened – or so he thought. The truth was he should have listened to Gwenyth. An hour or so later after making many more adjustments and still 'nothing happened', he went down to the basement studio. There were a few reference books there, which he thought might help him. Oh dear! What a shock! His favourite armchair and telescope were not there. As he looked around the room he noticed that his magnifying glass and binoculars were also missing.

When the surroundings had finally stabilised she was still sitting on the armchair but in a different point in time. The walls and ceiling of the studio had been left behind in the twenty-first century, as indeed had her home and the rest of the street. Gwyneth and her possessions were now situated in a forest. The Sun was shining and although it was a very warm day, the trees provided ample shade. Her first thought was about shelter. She knew that there were caves in the area. It was not long before she located one and, became acclimatised to her new surroundings. At night she took note of the positions of the stars, so she realised that she was now living about the time of the Viking invasion.

One day she met a boy in the forest. "Who art thou and from whither comest thou?" said Dennis Gwyneth thought for a while before answering. She decided that she would pretend to be the daughter of Minerva – one of the Witches she had read about in her favourite book. "I am Gwyneth – what is your name? And please don't tell the grown-ups about me",

"I am called Dennis – but thou speakest with a strange tongue."
"I talk English with a different dialect to you."
"Why art thou afraid of the grown ups."
"Because some may know that I am the daughter of Minerva who they say was a Witch."

~ ~ ~ ~ ~ ~ ~ ~ ~ ~ ~ ~ ~

"Grandpa – I thought it was only in the Bible people spoke 'thee' and 'thou' and that sort of English."
"Not so Jake, it was only about two hundred years ago or maybe even less that we stopped using 'thee and 'thou'. I'm sure your English teacher would know the exact date."
"Is it much further to the top of the tower Grandpa?"

"Don't tell me you're feeling tired Jake! When I was your age I could walk and climb for hours on end – it must be all that junk food you youngsters eat."
"What happened then Grandpa?" Jake did not want to get into an argument – he just wanted a short rest.
They stopped climbing, Grandpa smiled and said "Now where was I – oh yes Dennis asked Gwenyth."

~ ~ ~ ~ ~ ~ ~ ~ ~ ~ ~ ~ ~

"Where be thy mother now?"
"I don't know – they came from the castle and took her away."
"And thy father what of him?"
"I never knew him – mother never spoke about him?"
"Didst thou not ask thy mother about him?"
"Yes but all mother would say was one day I shall tell you"

Dennis felt tears welling up – in a soft voice he asked Gwyneth "Dost thou liveth here alone in the forest? From whither comest thy food?"
"I live off wild berries and herbs. My mother showed me from where I can gather and what to look for."
"And where sleepeth thee at night? Where ist thine abode?"

"Alas, after my mother was taken away they came again from the castle and burned down our hut. So I sleep here in the forest."
"But when it raineth and the snow falleth where shelterest thou?"
"I can't tell you for my mother made me promise not to tell of our secret place."

"But dost thou not haveth family or friends?"
"No, I am all alone in the world."
Dennis, who was very kind and tender hearted blurted out "Gwenyth – if I wouldst bring thee bread and milk wouldst thou think of me as thy friend?

Gwyneth stepped back. "Why would you want me as a friend?"
Because thou art a nice girl and I have not many friends – I like thee Gwenyth and wish to helpeth thee."

"How do I know that you will not give me away to the grown ups? Can you prove to me that you are trustworthy?
"Show me a place where I canst place down the bread and milk, and I willst bring them to that place each day."

Gwenyth thought for a while and then pointed to a large Oak tree nearby "When the Sun is high place the food in the hollow of that Oak. I will collect it later after you go."
Dennis agreed and so each day for the next week he would bring the bread and milk – each in its own wooden bowl and leave it in the hollow of the Oak tree. Gwenyth would remain hidden until she was sure that Dennis had not brought any grown-ups with him.

What Dennis did not know was that Gwenyth was able to spy on him from the edge of the forest and could track his path to the village.

It was sometime after their first meeting that Gwenyth felt that she could trust Dennis not to inform any adults of her presence. So one day after Dennis had left the food and was making his way back home he suddenly heard a voice call out "Dennis! Dennis come back I want to talk to you."

Dennis stopped, turned round but could see no one. He called out "Is that thee Gwenyth? Where art thou? I see thee not." Gwenyth called out "It's me, return to the Oak tree." Dennis did as he was told. However when he reached the Oak tree there was no one to be seen. For a brief moment Dennis did not know what to do. Then, once again the voice called out "I'm behind the large thicket. – come toward it." Dennis looked this way and that – there were a number of thickets to choose from – there was one that did seem a little larger than the rest so very slowly he walked towards it. Just before he reached it, out stepped Gwenyth. "Thanks for the food." Dennis smiled and said "I think that next time I'll bring thee some fruit if thou wouldst like. "I'd like that, but for now follow me to a small brook." She took him by the hand and led him deep into the forest. Dennis had never been so far into the forest and, although he did not show it he felt a little nervous.

It was a very hot summer day and he was beginning to feel thirsty. Then suddenly there it was a small brook. He let go of Gwenyth's hand and dashed towards the brook. He threw himself forward onto his stomach, put his face into the cool water and drank.

Gwenyth was soon by his side and she too drank from the brook. She shared the bread Dennis had brought her and he too ate a lump. They seated themselves comfortably, smiled at each other and Gwenyth said. "Can you see up the hill from where the brook's water comes? We must climb there – and I'll show you where I live."

Dennis looked up and saw a small hillock that was very steep. "Surely tis not possible to ascend such a steep hill."

"It's difficult which is why my mother chose it as our secret hiding place. But if you look along the line of trees that reach to the top of the hill, you will see the way we will climb."

A wave of fear crept over Dennis. He thought if Gwenyth's mother had made a secret hiding place – maybe she was a witch after all and Gwenyth too was a witch. What would happen to him if he entered the hiding place? He felt very sad because he liked Gwenyth a lot.

He decided to ask her why did the men at the castle think that her mother was a witch.

"It was because of the magic glass that came to her from out of the sky. I'll show you when we reach where I live."

So off they went. Gwenyth led the way. For a short while it was a fairly easy climb between rocks. They reached a tall Sycamore tree that had low branches.

"Wait a few moments till I call you." She lifted herself onto the lowest branch and heaved herself up to a much higher branch. She then uncoiled a rope that had been wrapped around an even higher branch.

She called out to Dennis. "Dennis I shall lower a rope – use it to pull yourself up."

Dennis was not used to climbing trees and it took some time before he reached Gwenyth.

"You are very slow Dennis but you'll get better." She laughed. She continued, "We must go on very slowly and take great care. See the large bough above – when we reach it you will see another bough on the Silver Birch tree. Then we must climb on to the

Silver Birch up a few more branches and from there we will step onto a ledge that is near the head of the brook.

Dennis did not want to go any further, but he dare not say so because he would feel very upset knowing that a girl was braver than him.

Before going on further Gwenyth lifted up the rope and wrapped it around the branch. "I must make sure that no one else will see it."

It took about ten minutes for them to reach the ledge. Dennis noticed large roots of many trees. However there was gap between two of the trees large enough for one person to go through. He saw a large shrub that was set well back from the ledge.

Gwyneth went forward, pushed the outer branches of the shrub, and there was an opening. Whilst still holding the back the branches she called Dennis over to join her. Dennis found himself in a cave. There was just enough daylight coming through the branches of the shrub. When his eyes got used to the semi-darkness he noticed some very strange objects on the ground.

"What are these?" he asked Gwenyth in amazement

"I don't know their names, but I know how to use the them."

"With this magic glass I can make fire."

"Surely thou jesteth with me Gwenyth." Said Dennis "Tis only with flint stones that we canst maketh sparks for fire."

"With this magic glass I can bring fire from the Sun – let me show you" Gwenyth picked up the magnifying glass and asked Dennis to move the branches at the cave entrance. Dennis did not move.

His earlier fears retuned. "Thinkest me that maybe the next time I cometh here, then thou canst showest me." His voice trembled as he spoke.

"Dennis what is the matter? You sound afraid. Surely you don't think I am a witch." Her voice was soft, sad and she began to cry.

"Well no it is not that." Said Dennis sounding uncomfortable. "I knowest not what to think – thou speakest of strange things that grown ups would sayest is the Devil's work – and yet because I liketh thee I wanteth not to think badly of thee."

"Maybe it would be better if we did not see each other again" Said Gwenyth sadly. She was suspicious that out of fear he would tell the adults of her presence.

"No Gwenyth no. We are friends – it be just that all this magic filleth me with fear."

"There is no need of fear Dennis – trust me." So once again Gwenyth asked Dennis to move the branches at the cave entrance.

Still feeling a little frightened Dennis did what he'd been asked. The Sunshine filled the cave with light. Gwenyth lifted the magnifying glass and moved it so that the Sun's rays were focused on a small pile of dried grass.

Dennis could not believe his eyes. First, smoke coming from the pile of grass and, seconds later, the grass burst into flame. Dennis's eyes were wide open in wonderment.

Before he could say anything Gwenyth said. "Would you like to see something even more magical?"

Dennis, who was still amazed by what he had just seen, nodded his head.

Gwenyth handed to him the pair of binoculars. She showed him how to use them.

"I'll hold back the branches then look in the direction of your village and tell me what you can see."

It took a while before Dennis was able to focus – but when he finally succeeded he shouted out in excitement "I canst see my father working in the field. There are soldiers from the castle walking in the village."

For about ten minuets Dennis spoke as fast as he described what he saw, that suddenly he was panting and gulping.

"Enough Dennis!" said Gwenyth laughing "Soon you'll have no breath left."
Dennis smiled and handed back the binoculars. "T'is all so amazing T'is unbelievable."

"There are more wonderful things Dennis." Gwenyth picked up a torch and using the magnifying glass she set it alight. She turned to Dennis and asked him to pick up the telescope.
"Follow me and take care for we go further into the cave. In time we will reach another opening near the top of the hillside."

They had not been walking very long, when they came to a fork in the ways.
"We go left Dennis – perhaps you would like to rest a while, I know that the long magic glass is heavy."
"Tis not so heavy – for a man that ist – I haveth not need of rest."
Said Dennis a little boastfully.

They continued walking. Dennis noticed that the path had become steep and the cave felt damp. After a while he could see faint daylight coming from way ahead.

"Is it much further, I seest daylight yonder."
Dennis felt tired but felt that he should not say so. He did not want Gwenyth to think him weak.
"It won't be long now Dennis we are very nearly there."

When they eventually reached the opening Dennis was pleased that he could sit and rest. It was much larger than the other cave entrance. Although it also was well hidden by a thick shrub. They left the cave and walked on. It was a rocky hillside with many large boulders. "When we reach the brow, we will then use the magic glass."

From the hilltop they could see the castle in the distance atop another hill. Dennis put the telescope to his eye. He spent some time looking at the castle. He could not see very much, although he saw the Blacksmith working at his forge.

He then looked in the opposite direction. What he saw he did not recognise. He turned to Gwenyth and said. "Knowest thou what it be at the foot of the far hills yonder?" Gwyneth smiled, "Tell me what you think it is?"

"Tis all a puzzle – I seeth a great amount of what looketh like water and there are objects resting upon the water."

"Dennis you are looking at the mighty sea, and the objects are ships."

Dennis gasped "The Sea! Ships! I must look again. Never didst I ever thinketh that I a son of a country peasant wouldst ever gazeth upon the sea."

"Why not Dennis? Asked Gwenyth in amazement, "It wouldn't take so long to reach the sea shore."

"The Baron at the castle does not let peasants leave the village. T'is a wonder to me that thy Baron let thee leaveth thy Village."

"Our Baron is very kind to us" said Gwenyth smiling.

Dennis raised the telescope to his eye and this time he made note of two flags that were flying on the shoreline. One was white with a red, two-headed bird. The other, green with a red dragon. He also noticed many soldiers, and many Horsemen. He would have liked to stay on the hilltop and observed a lot longer, but Gwenyth pointed out that the Sun would soon be setting and they should start making their way back.

"Very well Gwenyth, but we must cometh here again and looketh upon the sea."

They made their way back. When they reached the fork in the paths Dennis asked Gwenyth where did the other way lead to. Gwenyth said she did not know. She had once started out on that path, but it seemed to go on forever.

It was very late when Dennis arrived home. Already it was twilight.

"Where hast thou been till now?" Demanded his father. "Thy supper ist already on the table."
"I wast in the forest father and didst clamber hither and thither and noticed not the Sun goeth down."
"Be thou more attentive in future lad – now sit thee down and eatest thy bread and turnip."
Dennis was very hungry and ate much faster than normal.
His father said, "I seeth thy climbing giveth thee a big appetite, just where wast it thou wast climbing?"
"Up some trees and up the hill near the large oak father." Said Dennis.
He continued to speak "Father do thou knowest of soldiers who marcheth under a banner that ist white and has a bird that ist red and hast two heads?"

His father and mother both stopped eating. They stared at Dennis and looked very serious. "Why asketh thou such a question? Surely thou canst not have seen fighters carrying such a banner."

Dennis felt uncomfortable. He sensed that his parents were alarmed.
He wasn't sure how to explain the reason for his question. If he told them about Gwenyth and the magic glass, either they would not believe him or, they would be angry because they might know about 'Minerva the witch'
He decided that he would tell the truth.
"Father will thou promise that thou will not vent thine anger upon me if I tell thee all that has happened to me this day. I sweareth that all my words are the truth so help me."
His father assured him he would not be punished. His mother took his hand – and so he told them all that had happened that day and how he first met Gwenyth.

When he finished speaking his mother embraced and hugged him. She turned to her husband and said, "The witch's daughter has put a spell on him – Husband what canst be done to remove this wickedness so that our most beloved son be well again?"

"Be silent woman – walls have ears." He arose from the table and paced the floor. "Even if our son is bewitched he could be telling the truth because the fighters who wear the two headed bird are Northmen plunderers. And the red dragon men belong to the Baron of the western hills. If they be going to fighteth as one army." He did not finish his sentence. He sat down at the table, a grave expression on his face.

He turned to face Dennis and said "Telleth me again about the shape of the boats." Dennis did as his father asked.

His father said "Now show me just where thou wast and in which direction thou wast looking. Use the food bowls as markers. Show me the position of the Sun and the direction which the soldiers marcheth."

Dennis once again did his father's bidding.

His father spoke to his mother "There ist a landing point about three days march from here. The boy's markers show he speaketh truly even though he may have been in a witch's trance."

"So what canst be done?" asked Dennis's mother "Should we speaketh to the men in the castle?" . . . .

"Then what happened?" Jake asked his grandfather.

"There are many legends about that – next time we'll talk again."

Cinderella – The Truth

Thomas was fed up. The prince once again had fallen for a pretty face. "Don't come back until you find the beautiful vision of loveliness, whose perfectly shaped foot fits this glass slipper. Remember Thomas – I don't care how long it takes you must not fail."

"You'll have a right easy, well paid job at the palace" He recalled his father saying.

Thomas had wanted to be a computer technician, father was insistent. So now, here he was, tired, worn out and footsore walking the length and breadth of the Kingdom clasping a fragile glass slipper, knocking on doors. Like an out of work shoe salesman. It might not have been so bad, had he been given permission to travel by taxi. Oh no – the Prince thought that the engine vibrations might shatter the glass.

As time went by Thomas's appearance gradually deteriorated. The Inn-Keepers looked askance at the travel document bearing the Royal insignia and the Prince's personal seal. "Do you really expect anyone to believe that a tramp like you could possibly be an emissary from the Palace? – On your way and take that forged document with you – go on before I call the Police."

The bank manager listed patiently to his story – he refused him an advance. "How can you prove that this document is genuine?" Thomas had reached the end of his tether. Proof! You want proof" – just tell me what your collar size is."
'How will my collar size establish proof?"

"Simple!" said Thomas "When the Prince finds out how you've been treating me he'll have you beheaded and the executioner will want to know which size axe to use."

The bank manager strummed his fingers on the desk. "I am rather busy just now – can you come back in say about six months time? Oh you can leave the door open on your way out, goodbye and thank you for calling."

Thomas stormed out – "You live to regret this! Just you wait and see." Not far from the bank, Thomas came by a street where some imposing houses were situated. He went up the driveway of the first house and rang the bell. The door opened and there – in all her ugliness stood 'Miss Picasso model'.

"Who the hell are you buster?" she growled. Thomas explained who he was and why he had called.

"So, you are from the prince and you want us to try on a glass slipper." She turned her head and called out "Gladys, Millicent come here now – we have a real cookie weirdo at the door."

Thomas gulped. The two other women were undoubtedly sisters of Salvador Dali. Thomas explained his mission. They did not believe him.

They joined hands and made a circle around him and sang in non-melodious voices "He says he is from the palace and has a glass shoe. What are we going to do with him whatever shall we do."

So louder and louder they sang and faster and faster they danced. Eventually they ran out of breath and stopped dancing. Thomas, tired and bewildered asked with a croak "Are there anymore ladies in the house?"

The sisters looked at each other. Off they went again – dancing and singing "Anymore ladies in the house glass slipper man wants to know. Let's make him see Cinderella to the kitchen he will go."

By the time they stopped moving, poor Thomas was feeling dizzy.

The sister called out in unison "Cinderella – get in here now – you lazy good for nothing wretch."

The kitchen door opened and in walked a bedraggled young girl, mop bucket in hand. "I've —
"Stop talking when we've got something to say. – Give this daft excuse for a man a bowl of gruel. Then throw him out. If he tries to sell you a pair of glass shoes hit him with a large frying pan."
Thomas followed Cinderella into the Kitchen. "Sit down there."
She pointed to an old wood chair. "Anyone would think I've nothing to do – now I'm expected to feed a tramp. – What the hell did you come here for anyway?"

Thomas told her and showed her the glass slipper. Cinderella listened, a blank expression on her face. There was a long silence. "Do you really expect me to believe such a load of tosh?"
Thomas became angry. "Look here girlie – I've had my orders. You will try on this slipper and if it fits you'll be coming with me – cappiche? Okay?"
With that he stood up and in a determined manner advanced on Cinderella. She ran toward the kitchen range and grabbed the frying pan. Before she had chance to raise it Thomas grabbed her and wrested the Pan from her hand.

"Right – sit down – put on this slipper or I'll." He didn't finish his sentence but raised the pan menacingly over her head. Cinderella, nervously did as she was bid. The slipper fitted. Thomas dragged her out of the chair. "Okay girlie – you're coming with me – is there a back door out of here?"

Cinderella was in a panic. So she decided to play along with him. Once outside she could make a break and run off. "You don't have to be so rough – the back door's this way – please let go of my arm you're hurting me."

"No chance girlie – when we're at the palace – then I'll let you go, but not until."

They climbed the cellar kitchen stairs, Cinderella protesting and Thomas scowling. Then a stroke of luck . . . Thomas spotted one of the palace limousines flying the royal pendant. As it approached he recognised Buttons at the driving wheel.

Buttons couldn't believe his eyes. "You sir release that young maiden immediately or you'll have me to contend with"
"Buttons – you idiot it's me Thomas." He waived the glass slipper in front of Button's face. "This bimbo fits the slipper – help me get her in the car."
Buttons looks at Thomas, and approaches Cinderella. "There, there young lady have no fear I shall protect you from this dirty villain."
Thomas by this time to say the least is not feeling at his best. "There there young lady." Mimicked Thomas "For heavens sake open the rear door – I'll sit in the back and try get some sleep – here take the glass slipper."

"Good Lord! It is you Thomas. How on earth did—?"
"Never mind that now – just drive me and the Bimbo to the palace."
Buttons phoned the palace with the good news. The King ordered them straight to the Throne room.
"You have done well Buttons. I now have the lady I desire. This means promotion. But as for you Thomas – you dare to enter my throne room looking like a vagabond – why can't you follow Buttons example?"

THE END

Them Next Door

'I'm Jack and you are?

'Harry – Harry Marks. What's the grub like here?'

'Its edible – that's about as good as it gets. I must say Harry you don't look old enough to be in an old people's home.'
The sound of pleasant music and the sunshine falling into the Day Room put Harry in a good mood. Looking around he spotted a chess table and a box.

'Do you play Chess Jack?'

'I do – but no one else here does. So I'm right out of practice.'

'Okay – do you fancy a game? Though you should know I'm a very good player.'

'That sounds like a fighting challenge. I'll set them up.'
As the game proceeded, a usual Chess talk conversation came to an end. Jack took the opportunity to satisfy his curiosity. 'If you don't mind me asking Harry, How come you look about forty? Did you spend your entire spare time at the gym?'

'No – I'm a Magician.'
The bland serious tone in Harry's vice threw Jack into momentary confusion.

'I suppose travelling around the country going from one children's party to another and stage work must have been exercise enough.'

'No Jack – I *am* a *real* Magician. Oh by the way that was a wrong move – do you wish to take it back?'

The natural pride of all chess players would not allow Jack to reconsider.

'No I will stick.'

'In that case I must tell you that in twenty moves it's checkmate.'

'You can see twenty moves ahead?!!'

'I told you I'm a Magician – this situation is like a game that Capablanca played in the Twenties.'

Jack at this point wondered – was Harry's outlandish remarks a chess player's psychological attack on his opponents? If so – he could counter attack.

'When did you realise you were a Magician?'

'Not really sure. I suppose I should have cottoned on when I was at Primary school.'

'What Happened?'

'It was like this –'

. . . .

'Harry Marks you sit there in the front row of the class with your big brown eyes gazing into space looking so intelligent – deceiving us all.'

'That was my teacher's opinion of me. He divided the class into five groups A, B; C, D, and Mugs Alley. I was put in Mugs Alley. You can imagine just what a downer that was for me. Then the following day we were lining up for assembly, all of a sudden a man wearing a big black hat and cloak, burst in—I remember his long flowing white beard – he ran up and down the hall. When he saw me he stopped and thrust a bag of buns into my hand and said 'Eat, you will be blessed'.

By this time the Staff, who had been chasing him finally caught up with him and he was ejected out of the hall. I just managed to eat one of the buns when a teacher grabbed the bag from my hand.' Could be poisoned – you haven't eaten anything?'

'No Sir' I lied. 'Anyway, later in the day during Maths, we were set six problems and given the whole period – about an hour, to finish. I completed the lot in less than five minutes.'

. . . . .

'Harry Marks – don't just sit there. Make an effort. Try harder.'
'I've finished sir.'
'Finished? Finished!! Don't be ridiculous Marks.'
'Its true sir – The questions were not difficult at all.'

. . . .

'By this time all the class was staring at me and the teacher. I took my answer paper to him. You should have seen his face! Eyes bulging, mouth open. He sat back in his chair.
Muttering I don't believe it. I think he was conscious of all the class looking at him.
In a low voice he murmured 'All correct' Then in a loud voice – for the benefit of the class 'Try be a little more neater Marks – go back to your desk.'
    'So was that the moment of change for you?'
    'No – It was probably when the new neighbours arrived.'
ccccccc

    'What are you looking at Cynthia? You've been staring out the window nigh on twenty minuets.'
    'Why? Am I disturbing you?'
'No – you're just blocking out my light – I can't see to write. Anyway what's so fascinating out there?'
'I want to see our new neighbours.'
'You *know* for a fact they'll be here this afternoon?'
'Yes, Sue told me during our final chat. I'm so sorry she and Clive are leaving. Good neighbours are hard to find.'
'You're right there—but there's no point just standing and staring. You're bound to notice when the removal vans arrive.'

'They are cutting it fine – it'll soon be dark and – hello what? Come and have a look at this.'

. . . . .

'Do you remember those Messerschmitt Bubble cars Jack?'
'Not Half – I had one for a few years.'
'Anyhow – one drew up next door and out stepped a middle aged couple. They left it parked in the road and went into the house. My wife Cynthia seemed to be in shock.'

. . . .

'Crikey – they're both about six feet tall. How did they get onto that little thing?'
'I was thinking that myself. Can't worry about that now. I've got to finish off this article and the deadline is closing in. Why don't you go and introduce yourself.'
    'You must be a mind reader. See you in a bit.'

. . . .

'She must have been there at least an hour. When she came back she looked perplexed and never said a word. This for my wife is an unnatural state. I wasn't going to prompt her into verbal mode because I had still one more paragraph to finish.'
    'So did she eventually say anything?'
    'Yes – but not until I'd finished the article. I was feeling comfortable, relaxed and ready for the verbal onslaught.'

. . . .

'So tell me what do they call them? Did you warn them about the car thieves?'

'I asked them if they would like to come round to us for a cuppa. Instead they invited me for a sit down meal.'
'You mean they wanted to go out for a meal?'
'No.'
'You've been there over an hour – I don't understand, what –'
'They made a full chicken dinner with all the trimmings – including wine'
'I thought you sounded a bit tipsy. Just a minute, I remember Clive told me their cooker was on the blink and it was disconnected.'
'You think that was strange – you should have seen the beautiful dining room furniture!'
'How much wine have you had? I saw the removal men take away Sue and Clive's furniture. In fact when I popped round to say goodbye the house was virtually bare.'
'You think I don't know that? But I wasn't sitting on thin air during the meal. I'm not stupid.'
'Of course not. Did you mention about the car thefts and vandalised vehicles.'
'Yes. They told me not to worry. If there is any more trouble *he* will sort it out.'
'So what are their Names?'
'Mr and Mrs Kadmony. Adam and Evelyn. – Oh before I forget like you he is interested in Creative writing and asked if you fancy a game of snooker sometime tomorrow.'

. . . .

'You look tired Jack shall I shut up and –'
'Good lord no. I'm trying to avoid defeat as well as listening to your intriguing story.'
'Okay – but tell me when you've had enough. Anyway during the early hours of the next morning about three thirty or four.'

. . . .

'Sod me! What the hells all that screaming?'
'Eh! What? I'm trying to sleep. What's all the commotion?'

. . . .

'That was my wife once she starts snoring she could sleep through an earthquake. Well I went to the window and I don't mind telling you without exaggeration, I've never been so shocked. What looked like a giant black Panda – at least four times larger than normal – snarling and growling over three blokes their faces dripping blood .To cut a long story short by this time half the street was up. Soon the sound of Police car sirens were getting louder. Then as the Police drew up outside our house – the animal just disappeared. Next thing, the Police went from house to house to interview everyone.

. . . . .

'Harry – look who has just come out of next door!'
'I don't understand. They must be relatives. The last time I saw an ear trumpet like that was at an antique fair. I see the Cops have finished talking to them. They coming up the drive. Must be our turn to give evidence.'
'When did you realise there was a problem Mr. Marks?'
'I heard screams and a growling of an animal. I looked out the window and there was a monster Black Panther hovering over –'
'Quite so sir – your neighbours have said more or less the same thing. By the way – how long have known your next door neighbours?'
'Not long, they only moved in last night.'
'Might be a good idea to keep an eye on them. They seem a bit worst for wear. Old age and all that. I see you have a Neighbourhood Watch scheme here. So if you think they may need help give them a bell.'
'What about the wild animal on the loose?'

'We'll do what we can. For the moment just take extra care.'
'What's happening about the men who were attacked?'
'Ambulance should be here soon. We've been after them for a while. They are the Car Thieves.'

. . . . . .

'I was going to nip round next door there and then, but Cynthia decided we needed to go for a walk. So my visit did not take place till the following morning. It was then the moment of realisation that my life was about to change for ever.'
Jack, thinking that all he had heard so far was 'Chess players' psychological warfare' – made a mental note that no way was he going to be defeated. So, whilst working out a Stalemate strategy, he blandly asked 'How so Harry?'

. . . .

The sound of heavy rainfall lashing against the windows woke Harry just before his alarm clock was about to disturb his sleep. So, staggering from bed to window ledge, eyelids struggling to remain open, down went his hand onto the alarm stop. Cynthia, still snoring loudly as ever, gave Jack the chance to move quickly into the back bedroom before washing and dressing.
Drawing the curtains back and observing the downpour, looking right than left, grabbing a towel and was just about to head for the bathroom when he realised something was wrong.
Not quite awake, he couldn't fathom out where or what.
  Then, blurting out 'Sod me!' Dashing back to the window looking out in total disbelief at the next door back garden. Bathed in sunshine Adam and wife were sunning themselves. Head spinning in shock, trying to plan what to do after breakfast – should he wake Cynthia? No—the less she knows the better for marital stability. So whilst shaving he made what he called an

executive decision. A quick bowl of cornflakes followed by a visit next door.

Shouting from the bottom of the staircase 'Must dash beloved one, got to hand in the article.'

The response was 'I'm not awake – stop shouting 'Snore Snore, snort snort !!!

'Come in Harry. Fancy a coffee or tea maybe? I'm right in thinking you like Snooker, yes?'

'Tea would be nice – oh and yes I do like snooker.'

'Fancy a game.'

'I wouldn't say no. but the nearest snooker hall is on the other side of town.'

'We can play here. I have a table in the back room.'

. . . .

'I thought he meant a quarter size table. Where I lived the houses are very small cottage style. So you can imagine how shocked I was to see a full sized snooker table. That and the sunshine only shining over *their house* made me think perhaps I was hallucinating.'

'Look Harry before we start playing there is something you should know.'

. . . . .

'What he told me Jack at that moment was the beginning of a life change. Or should I say an explanation of how I became from a Mugs Alley dumbo to a real bright spark.'

. . . .

'Harry – have you ever study mysticism?'
'Not in any great detail'

'Well – all human beings are variations of the forty nine attributes as determined by the Sefrotic pathways between the worlds. I see you looked puzzled. In your case you are a rare person who via the line of Creation and the line of making that is *also* connected to the tree of knowledge of Good and Evil.'

'I'm sorry Adam – I am totally confused.'

'Tell me Harry did you enjoy the bun you ate in Primary School?'

. . . .

'He then went on to explain that if I were to write fiction all the characters would come to life. I asked him about the old couple who spoke with the Police. They were *His invention.* Likewise the giant Panther that attacked the car thieves.'

Jack, looking at the chess board knew that he could not force a stalemate, convinced himself that Harry's story was just a load of bunk used to distract him. And damn him – he had succeeded. Trying not to sound irritated, he asked,' So what did you do with your new found power?'

'I left the wife. Wrote for myself an ultra modern bachelor pad and every night for a month entertained a different long legged long haired blonde, Kinky boots black tights – the lot. Mind you after the thirtieth day was buckling at the knees – so I had to give them up'

'Harry do you think you could conjure up one those blondes for me?'

'Sure thing – anyway I must dash out now. Oh by the way that is checkmate. I'll arrange for some better food from now on.' With that he left the room.

'Good Morning Jack – who was that you were playing chess with.'

'An absolute nutter. If he's right in his head, we are all crazy. So any idea what muck we are having for lunch today Bert?

Before Bert could answer, a man dressed in full head waiters rigout entered and called out.

'Ladies and Gentlemen there is a change in luncheon times and menu. The first sitting will be in ten minutes. There are three choices. Venison, Steak Dianne. Or the vegetarian option Sweet potato with carrot salad. The side dishes are shown on the menus that waitress will bring you. Also there will be a bottle of champagne for each table. Thank you.'

'By the heck Jack what do you make of that?' Oh! Wow just look at that gorgeous dolly bird waitress serving the drink!'

'On reaching Jack and Bert's table the young lady asked 'which one of you is Jack?'

'Am sorry to say miss its not me' said Bert sounding sad and disappointed.

In a sultry voice that most men fantasise about she said 'I'm Sandra – I understand you are a chess player. I would like to learn. I'm told you know some interesting moves. I'm off duty at four o'clock' with a wink and a smile she went to another table.

Jack's sullen expression and general demeanour, Bert found bewildering to say the least.

'Is something wrong Jack? If I were you I'd be over the moon'

'This champagne is a bit off – I've tasted better.'

THE END

Overheard Remarks

Gentleman Jim

It was Detective constable Holdsworth's day off. He should have been at home with his wife. Instead he told her that he had something to finish off at the station and would be back after lunch.

Just so he was not technically telling her a lie, he did call in at the station. He went straight to his desk, opened one drawer, closed it and opened another. He removed a stapler, a few pens and a pencil.

It so happened that all his colleagues who were on duty were speaking into their respective telephones.

The Desk Sergeant gave him a quizzical look. Det.const. Holdsworth held up a sheet of paper as he made his way out.

The desk sergeant nodded as though he understood – and then continued doing whatever it was he'd been doing.

Once out the station Det.const. Holdsworth folded the sheet of paper; put it in an inside pocket and made his way to the high street. He entered the café opposite 'High Street Jewellers'. After obtaining a large mug of tea and a buttered scone, he seated himself at a table from where he could clearly see the entrance and shop front of the Jewellers.

He'd been on the case now for three days and still could not work out how 'Gentleman Jim' had managed to hide the stolen watches.

James Firthman was a well-known character to the local force. A very well spoken, immaculately dressed bowler hatted crook of the 'old school'.

Nine times out of ten the goods were recovered and usually he was let off with a severe warning. And nine times out of ten the police knew who the fences were who would receive his 'ill-gotten gains'.

If anything 'Gentleman Jim' was more of a nuisance than a criminal.

This time however the robbery was more serious. Diamond bracelet watches valued at more than £10,000 had been lifted in broad daylight. 'Gentleman Jim' simply walked into the shop – making sure that he was the only customer and had asked to see some diamond watches. It was a birthday present for his daughter, that's what he said to the assistant.

Whilst still looking at the pad of watches, he asked the assistant if he could look at a pad of brooches that were situated in a showcase behind the counter.

She turned around and removed the pad of brooches. When she turned to face 'Gentleman Jim' he was running out of the shop shouting "Dennis! Dennis! Hold on a second."

A short while later – a matter of a few seconds or so – he retuned to the shop and said to the assistant. "Would you believe it? I saw an old friend I've not seen for years and before I could attract his attention he'd hopped on a bus and I missed him."

In the meantime the assistant had noticed that three of the watches were missing from the show pad.

Before she could say or do anything the shop door opened and in walked the Manger, who bid a "Good Morning!" to no one in particular.

The assistant had a few words with the Manager and a while later the Police arrived and took 'Gentleman Jim' to the station for questioning.

He not only denied the accusation but insisted that he be stripped searched. His wish was granted. Apart from loose change and a few boiled sweets he was 'clean as a whistle'.

Det.Const. Holdsworth sipped his tea, stared out of the window and pondered. 'Gentleman Jim' works alone. Never been known to use an accomplice. So how on earth during the short period he was out of the Jewellers, manage to hide the goods?

"Harry Holdsworth aren't you supposed to be on a day off? What's up? Has she thrown you out then?" It was his friend P.C. Bill Williams who was taking a break from his regular beat.

"Throw me out! Never, she knows when she's on to a good thing."
"Yes well maybe – so why are you on your own and not with the lovely lady? Answer me that then D.T.Holdsworth?" said Bill grinning.

"If you must know it's that 'Gentleman Jim' case that's bugging me."
"I'll just get my cuppa and then I'll give you some advice." Bill went to the counter. As he was returning a voice from the back of the café called out "John go get your bike now we're going"
"It's not a bike dad."
"Well what ever it is get it – we're going now."
For some reason this short conversation stuck in Harry's mind. He was about to mull it over when Bill seated himself opposite and immediately started speaking and Harry lost his train of thought.

"If I were you Harry I'd phone 'wifey' and tell her you taking her for a slap-up lunch." Bill tone was serious. He continued "Family life is just as important as police work I've seen—"
The noisy entrance of four 'Yuppie types' drowned the rest of his sentence out
"Are you the 'A' team then?"
"We are a team – the trouble is Frank thinks he's in charge."
"So what do you care – as long as the job gets done."

Once again a glimmer of an idea presented itself in Harry's mind. And for the second time Bill's voice intruded on his thoughts.
"It's just not worth sacrificing your free time on a petty criminal like 'Gentleman Jim.'"

"Maybe you're right Bill." Harry took out his mobile and phoned home.
Bill stood up, smiled and left the Café – but not before giving Harry a 'Thumbs Up' sign of approval.

After spending a few minuets convincing his wife that he had not been up to anything untoward – she agreed to have lunch with him.

So a few hours later there they were in one of their favourite restraunts enjoying a first class lunch. Like all husbands Harry made one big mistake – he ordered wine.
"Wine! at Lunch Harry – you have been up to something. I want to know what it is.?" Mrs. Holdsworth's tone was one of incredulity and insistence.

Harry knew there was no point in protesting his innocence – so he decided to play along.

"You're right there has been something on my mind."
"I thought so – it wouldn't be that slim Blonde policewoman that you sometimes do the night shift with would it?"

"No of course not!"

"Why of course not – do walk around with your eyes closed?"

"You know I mentioned about that 'Gentleman Jim' case I'm working on – well it's annoying me. I know he's done it but I can't work out how."

"I take it you've not asked your Blonde night shift partner then?" she asked smiling – don't look so hurt I'm only teasing." She laughed.

"Tell me what the problem is – a fresh mind always helps."

Harry explained.
"It's obvious he must have had an accomplice." Said Mrs. Holdsworth
"Can't be – he always works alone."
"Why should this time be the same as the rest?" You should broaden your outlook." She continued "After all, if my husband, out of the blue suddenly decides to take me out to a posh lunch, then your 'Gentleman Jim' can be part of a team."

The word 'team' triggered off the overheard conversations in the café .
"Wait a minute – a child's bike – a child working with 'Gentleman Jim' that's the team." Harry almost shouted it out.
A few heads at the nearby table turned to look at him.

"Harry calm down – people are looking."
Harry calmed down, felt better than he had for nearly a week. He looked longingly into his wife's eyes and said "Darling you are a real treasure."

The following morning Harry went over the transcripts of his investigation. He looked up all the personal info on 'Gentleman Jim'.
There it was – he had a married daughter who had three children.

The question was – did anyone see a child riding a bicycle in the vicinity at the time of the robbery?

Harry made his way to the scene of the crime. He noticed that some shops had security cameras. Maybe one of them had film of the high street at the time of the crime.

Harry was right – after a number of discreet enquires – there it was 'Gentleman Jim' near a child riding a three-wheeler with a saddlebag.

"Good work Harry" said the Superintendent. "Trouble is the film is not all that clear and by now the stolen goods are probably out of the country."

"Couldn't I bring him in for further questioning?" Asked Harry seriously.

"No – it would be a waste of time and besides I need you on another case. Better luck next time."

The End

A day in the Country

Alan and Myrna Dakin are in the family car heading for Kirklevington. Myrna is driving.

MYRNA: So tell me again Alan – just how are you related to Denise? Marsden?

ALAN: How many more times do I have to repeat myself? Don't you ever listen to what I say?

MYRNA: I just want to be sure I don't say anything that might embarrass her.

ALAN: Okay for the third and last time – when I was young, happy and still single my Boss asked me if I was related to a Mr. Henry Berg.

MYRNA: (In a surprised tone) Your Boss? Why should he get involved with your family?

ALAN: Who's telling the story you or me? And will you keep your eyes on the road? Just drive and listen and don't interrupt.

MYRNA: Well excuse me I only asked a simple question.

ALAN: Okay but please don't ask any more just let me tell for the *third* time what you should know already. So as I was saying my Boss who was a pianist with a concert party was performing near Newcastle. Henry Berg was the violinist. During the interval they talked and during the conversation Mr.Berg mentioned that he was a Jewish refuge from Nazi Germany.

MYRNA: So where do you fit in to all this?

ALAN: If you'll give me chance to breathe and not interrupt I'll tell you.

MYRNA: Okay so get on with it.

ALAN: I would do but as usual you can't keep your mouth shut so I can't speak.

MYRNA: There's no need to be so rude. If you'd rather not tell me any more that's alright. You never talk to me anyway so why bother now?

ALAN: Why indeed? I'll read my book instead.

MYRNA: That's right – ignore me as you always do – I'm only your wife so why should you care about what I want?

ALAN: Alright – I'm sorry – would you like me to continue?

MYRNA: Only if it's not too much trouble for you. I wouldn't want to upset You.

ALAN: (With a deep sigh) So my Boss mentioned that he had a Jewish Apprentice who also played the violin. He also told him my name. Well Mr.Berg then said his father had told him that they had some distant relatives in England called Dakin. (A long pause)

MYRNA: So carry on – what next? How does Denise Marsden fit in?

ALAN: Wait a second – you are jumping the gun as usual. Anyway my Boss handed me a piece of note paper with Mr. Berg's address and phone number.

MYRNA: So what happened after you phoned him?

ALAN: You're at it again! I didn't phone him I wrote him a short letter.

MYRNA: Why? It would have the quickest way to contact him.

ALAN: You see what I mean – you never pay attention when I'm talking. If you'd have listened to me the last twice when I told you what happened you would have remembered that my parents were not millionaires and in those days trunk calls were expensive, whereas the cost of a postage stamp was not.

MYRNA: Did he reply to your letter?

ALAN: No he didn't, and as time went by I forgot all about the incident.

MYRNA: So how does Denise Marsden?

ALAN: I'm coming to that. Do you remember last Monday evening when you and your still unmarried nobody is good enough daughter were hogging the television gawping at East enders? Well –

MYRNA: There's no need to talk about Gillian like that – she's a good girl who makes good company for her mother and is very helpful around the home, this is more that I can say for her father.

ALAN: Well excuse me – I suppose shelling out for the household expenses mean nothing.

MYRNA: You're supposed to be telling about Denise Marsden – not criticising our lovely daughter.

ALAN: Okay – as I was saying – last Monday Gillian took a phone message from Denise Marsden.

ALAN: While you and Gillian were watching East Enders I phoned her back.

MYRNA: So what did she have to say?

ALAN: She said that she thought we could be related. Naturally I was surprised so I asked her for more details.

MYRNA: So then what happened?

ALAN: I'm coming to that – hold on a second – her grandfather was Henry Berg who had passed away a few weeks earlier. Whilst sorting out his papers and other things she came across the letter I'd written him over forty years ago.

MYRNA: I wonder why he kept it.

ALAN: Who knows – that's anybodies guess. The thing is she asked me if there was a possibility that were indeed related. Well as you know I asked dad's few remaining relatives about Henry Berg and they'd never heard of any Bergs in the family. Then the next thing that happened I'm listening to you making arrangements over the phone for to-day's visit, which I' still not looking forward to.

(FADE OUT TO A FEW DAYS EARLIER)

GILLIAN: Hi dad – Mom's on the phone in the front room.

ALAN: Evening Gillian – who she talking to?

GILLIAN: Don't know – oh we're eating in the front room.

ALAN: Okay I'll be quite as a mouse. Mustn't disturb Mom when she's in phone mode. (Sound of door opening)

MYRNA: It's very kind of you Denise – I'm looking forward to meeting you. We'll probably arrive sometime after lunch – anyway thanks again so until Sunday then bye. (Replaces receiver) You'll never guess who that was.

ALAN: Go on – surprise me

MYRNA: Well you know that lady who phoned you about a possible family connection—she's invited us to stay with them on Sunday.

ALAN: What do you mean? How can you stay for part of a day?

MYRNA: You know what I mean – stopover Sunday night – come back Monday.

ALAN: Why do you always do this to me? In the first place maybe I'll not be able to get time off work – and just maybe I may not want to go.

MYRNA: I can't go on my own – and besides what's so terrible about spending a few hours in the countryside?

ALAN: Okay supposing I can get time off – what do we do about Kosher food.

MYRNA: No problem – Denise and I have sorted it out.

ALAN: In any case why would she want us to visit?

MYRNA: She said there was a delicate matter she would like to discuss.

ALAN: So why not write a letter?

MYRNA: She said it was urgent and wanted to speak face to face rather than over the phone.

ALAN: I just hope that out of respect for our Kosher dietary laws we are not served steamed fish with boiled potatoes which is what usually happens when I'm asked to address Non-Jewish groups.

MYRNA: Well even if that is the case it won't do you any harm – steamed food is one of the healthiest foods.

ALAN: Be that as it may I still don't like it.

MYRNA: Don't worry I'm sure you'll survive and besides if the weather is nice you won't even notice the food.

ALAN: Checkmate – you win but in future don't accept any more invitations on my behalf.

MYRNA: Other Invitations! What other Invitations could we possibly receive? You never take me anywhere, we never go out – see anybody. All you want to do is change armchairs and stuff your face with cheese sandwiches.

ALAN: There's nothing wrong with cheese – it's very tasty and I like it.

MYRNA: I suppose you'd like me to ring Denise back and cancel.

ALAN: No of course not.

MYRNA: Are you sure – I wouldn't want you to go under sufferance.

ALAN: I'm sure – If the weather is nice it could be a pleasant change.

(FADE OUT TO THE CAR JOURNRNEY)

MYRNA: What do you mean – you're still not looking forward to it. I hope you're not going to just sit there looking bored.

ALAN: What I meant was I hope the delicate matter is not going to be complicated. I hate having to give advice.

MYRNA: You know your trouble is

ALAN: No – but I bet you're going to tell me.

MYRNA: The problem is you don't like people. You avoid them so if someone asks you a question you flap.

ALAN: What a load of twaddle. I – Just a second – we've just entered Stockton and that pub over there has lots of Parking spaces, so it shouldn't take you longer than an hour to decide where to park the car.

MYRNA: Very funny – I'd just wish you'd learn to drive – that would be a miracle.

ALAN: Drive! Not me no way I'd be so much better that you at it you'd never get over it.

MYRNA: Right I'm going to park here.

ALAN: You can't park here

MYRNA: Why not – it's ideal

ALAN: Can't be – this is the first spot you looked at and normally you change your mind at least three times.

MYRNA: Just get out the car. I need the Loo.

(THEY ENTER THE PUB. AT ONE END IS A JUKE BOX
AND A SMALL DANCING AREA)

ALAN: Shall we create a record? Can I pick a table without you not changing your mind three times before deciding which one?

MYRNA: Just pick one not too near the Jukebox.

ALAN: Okay I'm going to have a tomato juice – what do you want?

MYRNA: The same. (Goes off in search of the Loo – Alan goes to the bar humming the Dusty Springfield number in the Middle of Nowhere which is being played on the Jukebox He makes his way to the bar and orders)

ALAN: Two tomato juices please with ice and a dash of Worcester sauce.

GLENDA: (Approaching from behind – taps Alan on the shoulder) Hello handsome – fancy seeing you here

ALAN: Glenda! This is a pleasant surprise – what brings you here? It's good to see you again.

GLENDA: This is my local Harold and I sometimes come here for lunch on a Sunday – He's over there with the girls. (She points to a table – Alan waives)

ALAN: So how's life treating you?

GLENDA: We are doing okay thanks and how about you?

ALAN: Not too –

GLENDA: Our lunch is going to be a while yet – fancy a dance?

ALAN: Sure why not!

GLENDA: So what brings you to this neck of the woods?

ALAN: We're on our way to Kirklevington

GLENDA: Business or pleasure? – Oh I see our lunch is being served. Must go – nice seeing you again Alan. (Kisses him on the cheek) Enjoy your trip.

(ALAN TURNS AND MAKES HIS WAY BACK TO HIS TABLE ONLY TO SEE MYRNA SITTING THERE)

MYRNA: I see you're up to your old tricks again.

ALAN: Tricks! What tricks? I –

MYRNA: You know perfectly well what I mean – you did the same thing ten years ago at the charity dance – you can't behave yourself – you see a pretty woman and lose control.

ALAN: Hold on a minuet – let me explain

MYRNA: You don't have to explain – I know you and how your mind works.

ALAN: For your information the lady used to be my boss at the hospital. I've known her for years – and besides she's here with her husband and daughters

MYRNA: Did she really have to kiss you?

ALAN: It was only a way of saying goodbye in a friendly manner.

(BARMAID COMES OVER TO CLEAR THE TABLE)

BARMAID: Can I get you anything else to drink?

MYRNA: We'll have the same again – oh and can you fetch a bucket of ice which I'd like you to pour over my husband's head.

BARMAID: I'm sorry madam we've only got licences for liquor, music and dancing. Been up to no good as he? My old man's a gem of a fellla but I don't allow him out of my sight for longer than I have to. They are all the same even the best of 'em.

ALAN: Are we on the right road to Kirklevington?

BARMAID: Yes – you're not all that far – go out of the car park, turn left, pass through two sets of traffic lights. Then you see a big dress shop on the next corner, turn left and follow the signs to Yarm.

MYRNA: Is it worth while going to the dress shop?

BARMAID: It's a bit pricey. Quality's good though and there's a Sale on.

ALAN: Oh wonderful – a dress shop with a Sale on – the only thing in life worse than steamed fish. Do we really have time to shop?

MYRNA: Of course we do. I'll only be ten minuets. Anyway I don't know why you're complaining – who knows maybe they'll have a good looking blonde assistant who will also give you a goodbye kiss.

ALAN: Okay – shall we move off then?

(FADE OUT – THEN IN THE SHOP)

MYRNA: There's nothing here that I really like but I'll just look at this in the mirror. Here hold this one. Hmm what do you think?

ALAN: Well I –

MYRNA: Never mind – I don't why I bother asking you – you've got no taste.

ALAN: Of course – so why did you ask me?

MYRNA: There's nothing here I like. Come on lets go. (They reach the exit) I'll just go try that yellow top on again. You wait here I shan't be long. (A short while later she returns holding a yellow and a white blouse)

MYRNA: I'm not sure which one to buy. What do you think?

ALAN: Why don't you do what you usually do? Buy them both then on the return journey bring one back and get a refund.

MYRNA: Alan I'm being serious.

ALAN: I know – let me buy one of them – you buy the other. In that way when you decide you don't like the one I bought you can then turn round and say – I don't know why you bought me that thing – it doesn't suit me you are absolutely useless. Just think what pleasure you'll get saying that.

MYRNA: You're really not very helpful – can't you be serious just for once?

ALAN: Okay tell you what – I'll get them both on my credit card and then as I said – if you're not happy we'll pop in on the way back agreed?

MYRNA: Very well okay.

(FADE OUT – THEN)

ALAN: Well Myrna – who is the star navigator then?

MYRNA: I'll bet it was more by luck than judgement.

ALAN: Anyway here we are – and just look at that beautiful garden. Have you ever seen such large beautiful roses.

MYRNA: Very nice – now lets go inside.

(They leave the car and approach the door – the door opens and a girl about six years old and a Golden Retriever greet them).

CHARLOTTE: Mummy! Mummy they are here. Hello I'm Charlotte and this is Rover – he's very friendly (Pointing to the entrance) and that's Mummy.

DENISE: Please come inside – how was the journey?

ALAN: Very good thank you.

DENISE: Please make yourselves comfortable – I'm sure you'd like a drink what will it be tea or coffee?

MYRNA: We'll have tea milk no sugar thanks.

DENISE: And you Alan what would you like.

Alan: I should point out that when my wife says 'we' it is in the sense of the 'Royal we' so I would not dare asking for anything else.

MYRNA: Take no notice of him Denise – he always tries to make out that I'm some sort of ogre.

ALAN: I rest my case.

DENISE: I think I get The picture. Charlotte go and tell dad that our guests have arrived, he's in the back garden weeding the vegetable patch. I'll just nip into the kitchen and make the tea. Sharn't be long.

MYRNA: Now this is what I call a home. The décor is perfect, plenty of natural light and what beautiful furniture. It is so comfortable.

ALAN: Do you mean to tell me that you can find anything wrong with this place? Just who are you woman and what have you done with my wife?

MYRNA: Don't worry it's still me. We've only been here for five minutes or so

ALAN: Oh dear! And here am I thinking providence has sent me a new much improved better model.

MYRNA: Listen – just remember –

(ENTER GRAHAM DENISES'S HUSBAND)

GRAHAM: Good afternoon – I'm Graham and you must be Alan and Myrna. Delighted to know you. I'll just get out of these Gardening togs and join you in a jiffy. Here's Denise with some refreshments.

DENISE: Don't be too long darling – there's nothing worse than cold tea.

GRAHAM: How could I possibly when the aroma of your freshly baked scones fill the air – in the meantime show Alan the letter.

DENISE: (Hands Alan an envelope) Do you remember writing this Alan?

ALAN: Well, Well this takes me back. I was only fifteen when I wrote it.

MYRNA: May I see it? (Alan passes the letter) Your handwriting hasn't improved.

ALAN: I suppose Denise your Grandfather intended answering it at some point otherwise he wouldn't have kept it.

DENISE: Could well be. Shall I show you to your room so you can freshen up?

MYRNA: That sounds good to me I could do with a lie down after the driving.

DENISE: How does Strawberries and cream on the lawn in about an hour sound.

ALAN. Sounds great to me Denise.

GRAHAM: Here let me take your cases.

(FADE OUT)

MYRNA: My bed is so comfortable – how's yours?

ALAN: Just right

MYRNA: What time did she say for tea?

ALAN: Have a look at your watch – and please be silent for a while. I'm tired and want to relax – so shush.

MYRNA: Well I'm sorry if you can't be bothered to tell me the time because you are tired – you forget who does the driving in this family, all the driving because you can't make the effort to learn – and it doesn't occur to you that maybe I too might be feeling tired. I'm sorry if it means you getting off your bed and walking all the way to the dressing table. If it's too much trouble then –

ALAN: Alright! Alright! Keep your hair on – It's twenty passed nag-nag.

MYRNA: What did you say?

ALAN: I said it was twenty passed three my sweetness and life's delight.

MYRNA: (Throws a pillow at Alan) You really are horrible – why is it always too much trouble for you to do even a little thing for me?

ALAN: I'm glad the weather has kept fine – I wonder who looks after the roses – I'll bet they could win a prize.

MYRNA: Yes they are super maybe – (Sound of snoring)

ALAN: Wonderful – Twenty whole minuets of silent bliss.

(FADE OUT)

MYRNA: Have I overslept? What time is it Are we late? Where are we?

ALAN: No need to fret dearest – as usual in your ever efficient way you have woken up bang on time. I'll freshen up first. It'll give you time to come round.

MYRNA: Don't be too long.

ALAN: No problem – we still have a good ten minuets.

(FADE OUT)

GRAHAM: Here on the patio – strawberries and cream for the eating.

MYRNA: Sorry if we're a bit late – we were just admiring the garden from the bedroom window

ALAN: Who is the head gardener?

GRAHAM: For my sins I confess it's me.

MYRNA: You must spend a lot of time at it – it's an absolute picture. Have you won any prizes or anything?

GRAHAM: Denise is the only one who has won trophies for her roses.

MYRNA: You see Alan – where the best is needed – send for the women!

DENISE: Myrna you are absolutely right – but I must say Graham always does his best. Now who is ready for strawberries and cream?

ALAN: I'm certainly ready and I don't think Myrna will say no.

CHARLOTTE: Can I have some mummy please?

DENISE: As long as you eat your tea later on and not stuff yourself now.

CHARLOTTE: Promise! Promise! Promise! I'll only have a little.

GRAHAM: Go and bring a chair for yourself.

CHARLOTTE: Can I fetch Teddy as well?

GRAHAM: Why on earth do you want to bring teddy?

CHARLOTTE: I want him to meet our guests – I'm sure he'd like to meet them.

GRAHAM: Very well but you'll have to fetch another chair.

CHARLOTTE: Okay Daddy yippee! Back soon!

GRAHAM: Charlotte is very proud of her teddy. She won him at the funfair last year. He is very large, almost as big as her.

DENISE: Where was Charlotte dashing off to just now? She asked for strawberries and cream and now she's not here.

GRAHAM: She wants teddy to meet Myrna and Alan

DENISE: Her and that teddy – I'm so sorry she won it – she should spend more time doing her homework and practicing the violin instead of playing imaginary games with that bear

GRAHAM: Don't be too hard on her Denise. It's a phase all children go through – in the long run it helps develop their creative skills.

MYRNA: I see we have a daddies little girl situation here Denise.

DENISE: And does she take advantage of it

ALAN: Do you have any other children?

DENISE: Yes we have another daughter at University in Newcastle. There is a ten year difference between them.

GRAHAM: In point of fact it is Tracey our eldest that we want to talk to you about. You see – careful Charlotte don't run so fast Rover tries to keep up with you and they'll be an accident.

CHARLOTTE: I am being careful daddy – Teddy I would like you to meet Mr. and Mrs. Dakin. They are from Leeds.

ALAN: Shall I hold him while you bring your chair over

CHARLOTTE: Thank you. I'm sure teddy won't mind sitting on a stranger's knee – he's quite good that way. I'll just get his chair.

ALAN: Charlotte teddy has been telling me things about you and I must say I'm very surprised at what he told me.

CHARLOTTE: You're kidding me Mr.Dakin – teddy is a toy and toys can't speak.

ALAN: Oh yes they can Charlotte – you see when I was a little boy I had a teddy and he taught me.

CHARLOTTE: I can't believe that.

ALAN: I'll prove it to you Charlotte. I'll ask him again. Teddy is it true what you just told me about Charlotte? Teddy says you do not practice the violin as you should do. Do you playa violin Charlotte.

CHARLOTTE: Yes I do!

ALAN: And what's that you're saying about Charlotte teddy I'm surprised at you. I do not believe it. I'm positive that Charlotte always does her homework – shame on you teddy for what you just said. Charlotte is a good girl.

MYRNA: This is how he would carry on with our two when they were young.

ALAN: Would you play your violin for me Charlotte?

CHARLOTTE: I don't think it is in tune – I haven't been taught how to tune it.

ALAN: Well Charlotte I'm also a violinist so I'll tune it for you.

CHARLOTTE: Shall I get it mummy?

DENISE: Sure – run along.

(CHARLOTTE GOES INTO THE HOUSE)

MYRNA: You really shouldn't have done that Alan – you've upset her.

ALAN: On the contrary in years to come the fruits of my strategy will be apparent.

(CHARLOTTE RETURNS CARRYING A VIOLIN CASE)

ALAN: Denise was this by any chance your grandfather's instrument?

DENISE: Yes – I don't know how he got it out of NAZI Germany.

ALAN: Charlotte would you put it under your chin as though you were going to play it? Okay now put it down. Well Denise I can see why Charlotte is not enthusiastic about violin practice. It is much too large for her. If you don't mind me offering some advice, I would recommend that until she is a little older it would be a good idea for her to learn on a three quarter size instrument.

GRAHAM: The school never mentioned that – I am surprised.

ALAN: Charlotte what sort of instrument does your music teacher use?

CHARLOTTE: When he teaches a new tune he uses mine.

ALAN: I am not surprised – Graham, Denise – If I tilt the violin just so and you look inside via the slits in the front – look at the printing. Can you make it out?

DENISE: I've never bothered to look before. Wait a second I can just see make out the words – Von Shtubacher 1799

ALAN: Here Graham you have a gander as well.

GRAHAM: Good Lord! If I'm not mistaken wasn't he a famous instrument maker?

ALAN: Exactly my point – I don't wish to sound uncharitable – but I suspect Charlotte's music teacher enjoys playing this instrument.

DENISE: I'll bet that's the reason why he never mentioned that Charlotte would be better off playing a smaller size violin.

MYRNA: How do you known this is not just a copy instrument?

ALAN: Simple – May I play a few notes just to demonstrate Denise?

DENISE: By all means – please do.

ALAN: Actually even without playing a single note I can prove this is the genuine item.

GRAHAM: How so?

ALAN: Look here everyone – see this G string? It's made of cat gut like the others. This could well be the original string. Copy Von Shtubachers were not made until wire G strings came into use.

MYRNA: Does that mean we don't have to listen to the recital of the strangled cat after all?

ALAN: What! And disappoint my adoring public – never!

(PICKS UP VIOLIN – TUNES UP – PLAYS A FEW CHORDS THEN STRAIGHT INTO BRAHAMS HUNGERIAN DANCE No.5)

ALAN: Did you notice how resonant the lower pitched notes sounded? Von Shtubacher was noted for his low pitch instruments.

MYRNA: Well! Well! And here was I thinking it was your playing that was good. How wrong could I be?

ALAN: I'll bet Isaac Stern, Jasha Heifitz and Yehuda Menhuin never had to put up what I have to put up with

MYRNA: And they didn't have to pit up with you.

ALAN: is it insured by the way.

GRAHAM: It's covered by the general household goods policy.

ALAN: I know it's not in the same category as a Guneria or a Strad. But I would get valued. Mind you if I were you I'd insure it right away for at least Five thousand pounds, and that is a conservative estimate

GRAHAM: As much as that! – I'll get on to it straight away next week.

DENISE: Would anyone like more tea and scones?

ALAN: Yes please – you know Denise I could very easily get used to your garden and the sunshine – it beats working in an office. What do you say Myrna?

MYRNA: Absolutely – It's fabulous.

ALAN: You all heard that! – please make a note in your diaries – on this day at this hour Mrs. Dakin agreed unreservedly with a statement made by her husband. It is doubtful if such a phenomenon will ever again occur during the history of Mankind.

MYRNA: You could also note that the country air affected Mr. Dakin that he actually spoke more than one word at a time. He even, to his wife's consternation used whole sentences.

DENISE: I wonder if we could perhaps have our serious chat about Tracey.

GRAHAM: Yes I suppose now is as good a time as any. Charlotte take your ball and Rover and play at the far end of the garden please.

CHARLOTTE: What about teddy?

GRAHAM: I think he can stay. I'm sure he'll behave himself.

CHARLOTTE: I'm not that sure. I know I'll take him back to my room then come out to play – Come on Rover were just taking Teddy inside – here boy. (Exit Charlotte in to the house)

DENISE: I think you'd better begin Graham and don't be so dogmatic.

GRAHAM: Okay well her goes – Alan and Myrna if your daughter wanted to marry someone who wasn't Jewish would you approve.

MYRNA: To be honest until I'd be faced with such a situation it is very hard to know what the reaction would be.

GRAHAM: What's your view Alan?

ALAN: Like Myrna said because it hasn't happened I cannot say with absolute certainty one way or the other. However I'm ninety-nine percent sure that not only would I disapprove. I would take steps to that such a union would not take place.

GRAHAM: There you are Denise! My view exactly. Prejudice does not come into it.

DENISE: Well I'm sorry – I think it is prejudice. If two people really love each other why should the rest of the world interfere?

ALAN: Do I take it that Tracey has met a Non—Christian boy.

GRAHAM: I'm afraid so. And I do not want her to marry someone who is Jewish – No disrespect to you Alan and Myrna, but as a practicing Anglican Christian I want my family to continue in that tradition.

ALAN: That's perfectly understandable to me – it makes a good sense. Do you know what stage the relationship has reached?

DENISE: The truth is Tracey says she will convert to the Jewish faith and Graham is not happy with that. You see he is deeply involved with the Church. He's a Church Warden.

GRAHAM: Hang on a bit Denise! My objections have nothing to do with my church involvement. I'm only thinking of Tracey's well being and happiness as any responsible father would?

DENISE: I'm sorry Graham it doesn't sound like that to me. If you really loved her like you say then you'd give her your support and understanding.

ALAN: Have either of you met the boy? Do you know what his parents feel about the situation?

(ENTER CHARLOTTE BOUNCING HER BEACHBALL WITH ROVER)

DENISE: We don't even know his name or even if he has a family. Tracey says very little knowing how Graham feels.

CHARLOTTE: I know what they call Tracey's boy friend.

DENISE: Charlotte – How many times do I have to tell you. Don't tell lies and never listen-in to grown-ups conversations. Its bad manners and very rude.

CHARLOTTE: I wasn't listening in – everyone was talking loud so I couldn't help hearing.

DENISE; Even so Charlotte – you shouldn't be telling lies.

CHARLOTTE: But mummy I do know his name honest.

GRAHAM: Charlotte – please come here and sit on daddy's knee. I want to talk to you

DENISE (To Myrna) Daddy's little girl!

MYRNA: Same with us – Our Gillian is always right – according to Alan.

GRAHAM: How do you know what they call Tracey's boy friend's name. Did Tracey tell you?

CHARLOTTE: No daddy – I heard her speaking to him over the telephone one night when she thought I was asleep.

GRAHAM: So how did it come about and what is his name?

CHARLOTTE: Don't want to daddy – Tracey would kill me if she found out I'd split.

ALAN: Denise has Tracey mentioned anything at all about him?

DENISE: All she has mentioned is that he is twenty three, works in his father's garage in Newcastle. She wants to convert so they can get married.

GRAHAM: Myrna – do you remember the inter-Synagogue Quiz contest?

MYRNA: Of course – it was just over two years ago.

ALAN: If I remember rightly – it was the Newcastle team that came down to leeds.

MYRNA: You're right – they won the match.

ALAN: Now it's coming back. Their captain was a garage owner.

MYRNA: That's right – his wife looked like a horse. A tall skinny woman with no dress sense at all. She wore a horrible green out fit that made her look like a runner bean.

ALAN: By any chance do you recall their names?

MYRNA: Sorry – no.

ALAN: In that case It all depends on Charlotte. There is something at the back of my mind which I think may be significant.

MYRNA: How do mean significant?

ALAN: Without the name – I'd just be guessing.

GRAHAM: Charlotte go over to Mr.Dakin and tell him the name.

CHARLOTTE: But daddy – Tracey will be angry with me.

ALAN: Tell you what Charlotte – You whisper the name to Teddy and then teddy will whisper it to me. Go on Charlotte fetch teddy over to me.

(Charlotte complies)

ALAN: Thank you Charlotte – now I'll just put teddy's mouth to my ear like this – Now Charlotte whisper the name in teddy's ear.

CHARLOTTE: (In a loud whisper) Jeremy Khannman.

ALAN: Teddy would you mind repeating the name. Thank you teddy I'm much obliged to you.

DENISE: Charlotte – have finished all your homework?

CHARLOTTE: Not yet mummy – I'll finish it later.

DENISE: No Charlotte – now please – go inside and get on with it.

CHARLOTTE: Oh! Daddy – do I have to do it right now?

GRAHAM: I think you should do as mummy says Charlotte.

CHARLOTTE: Come on teddy we've been sent inside.

ALAN: Myrna – do me a favour please phone your Sandra and ask her if she can let me have details about the Khannmans belong to Newcastle synagogue.

MYRNA: How can you be so sure that's the family?

ALAN: Two reasons – one, because that's the name Charlotte – or should I say her teddy told me. And two, because during quiz contest I spoke to Mr.Khannman and he had a garage and I believe he mentioned that he was a Cohen but I'm not certain. I would like Sandra to confirm it.

MYRNA: My mobile is in the bedroom. I'll call her from there.

ALAN: You see Graham – Cohen is the Hebrew word for a Jewish Priest. A descendant of Aaron – it's in Exodus. Now if I'm right then there would be no point in Tracey getting converted because a Cohen is forbidden to marry a convert. Now my wife's sister is known as the Kosha nostra or the Yenta-net. Within twenty four hours I'll guarantee she have all the info. That was quick Myrna. Any luck?

MYRNA: Afraid not – The home number is on answer phone.

ALAN: Don't tell me *her mobile was engaged.*

MYRNA: No need to be sarcastic. I'll call a bit later.

ALAN: Yes I suppose you could do so – even *Sandra* must pause for breath even if it's only once a year. Anyway Graham when is it best to call during the week?

DENISE: Any time after six thirty. Tea will be ready in an hour – maybe you and Myrna would like to have a look at the village in the meantime.

MYRNA: To tell the truth I'd sooner stay in your lovely garden and soak up the sunshine – or perhaps I could give you a hand with tea.

DENISE: Whatever you like Myrna – we could have a woman to woman chat.

GRAHAM: In that I case I'll go with Alan to the village pub.

ALAN: Now that sounds very interesting.

(FADE OUT)

DENISE: That's good timing – how was the pub?

ALAN: It's just how I think a typical should be, quaint décor and a very good pint.

DENISE: Right then are you ready for poached salmon?

ALAN: One of my favourites – by the way did Myrna mange to contact her sister yet?

DENISE: I don't think so – her she is now

ALAN: Hi Myrna – any luck with Sandra.

MYRNA: Not yet – I left a message to call me back.

(MYRNA'S MOBLIE RINGS)

MYRNA: How's that for timing – hello Sandra – glad you phoned back – how are you – fine. Sandra Alan would like a favour regarding a Newcastle family. The name is Khanmann its spelt K, — What do you mean – with you – where are you calling from – just a minuet can you hold on?

ALAN: What's up what's the problem

MYRNA: They are with them now.

ALAN: Who is with Whom? You're not making sense.

MYRNA: The Khanmanns – who else have we been talking about? Sandra and Simon are visiting Harvey in Gateshead. The Khanmanns are visiting there youngest.

ALAN: I'm with you now – I take it they are both studying at the Yeshiva.

MYRNA: Of course where else.

ALAN: Is Simon there let me have a word with him.

MYRNA: Just a second – Sandra sorry about that – is Simon with you? Alan wants a word. (Hands the mobile to Alan)

ALAN: Simon – just a second – I think I'd better take the call in the bedroom

(FADE OUT)

MYRNA: What took you so long we're all starving here – so tell us what happened?

ALAN: I thought you were hungry – so what do you want to do eat or listen?

MYRNA: Just tell us what happened.

ALAN: Right this is the position. The Khanmanns have been worried about their eldest son Jeremy. He's been behaving out of character lately. very surly, irritable and snappy. He wouldn't tell them what's bothering him. Well to cut a long story short I explained about Tracey. And the upshot is Mr.Khanmann is now on the phone to his son and Simon will phone back as soon as he has any further news.

DENISE: I suppose that will take some time in the meantime let's eat.

MYRNA: Let me give you a hand serving Denise.

(FADE OUT)

ALAN: Denise that was delicious and the parsnip wine has a real kick. Compliments to the Chef.

DENISE: Glad you liked it.

(MOBILE RINGS)

ALAN: That must be Simon – Hello Simon what's the score? Ah Ha – I'm not surprised. Yes – and has he. Well I think the boy has behaved badly – It's a disgrace. I will – sure – you too – have a good week.

MYRNA: So tell us what's happened.

ALAN: Hang on a second! This is not going to be easy. I was right the Khanmanns are Cohenim. So what Jeremy Khanmann intended was to join the Reform.

DENISE: What does that mean exactly Alan.

ALAN: You know what the relationship is like in Ulster between the Protestants and Catholics – Well in the Jewish world the relationship is almost the same – but not as friendly.

MYRNA: What Alan means is the Reform don't accept any traditions and is more of a DIY interpretation of Jewish law.

ALAN: Well anyway the Khanmanns have relatives in Detroit and Jeremy will have to stay with them for at least two years otherwise Mr.Khanmann will disown him with a never darken my doorstep again and you'll be removed from my will syndrome.

MYRNA: Detroit – That's in America.

ALAN: Well what do you know! And there was I thinking it was just outside Heckmondwike. Of course it's in America. That's the idea. Two years apart the young couple are bound to meet someone else.

MYRNA: Wait a moment – do we know if Jeremy has agreed to go.

ALAN: What do you think? His father is going to make him a generous allowance – Detroit is the largest automobile centre in the world. As a mechanic he gets a job. He'll be living the life of Riley.

MYRNA: Yes – but do we know if he has agreed to go.

ALAN: Well of course he has. I wouldn't betting he's packing his bags right now.

MYRNA: There's no need to shout at *me* Alan. I only asked a simple question.

ALAN: I'm sorry if I sound angry. The truth is I feel sorry for Tracey. I feel she has been treated shabbily.

DENISE: I think I'd better make a start on the washing up.

MYRNA: I'll give you a hand Denise.

DENISE: Its okay you don't have to

MYRNA: Oh but I must – I need woman to woman contact only. Men can be so nasty at times.

(EXIT DENISE AND MYRNA TO THE KITCHEN)

ALAN: Glad I'm not young anymore. Love relationships are always bitter sweet. And in my case its usually more bitter than sweet.

GRAHAM: Sadly Tracey does not have the benefit of mature years.

ALAN: At least when her suitor gives her the elbow – as they say – you'll be prepared and have time to work out how to deal with it.

GRAHAM: Yes that's a point but it still won't be easy. What time do you and Myrna want to leave tomorrow?

ALAN: As soon as possible soon after nine-o-clock.

GRAHAM: We'll be eating breakfast at eight so that should give you plenty of time.

(FADE OUT TO ALAN AND MYRNA DRIVING
BACK TO LEEDS)

ALAN: Fancy a break in Harrogate for lunch rather than going straight home.

MYRNA: Sure why not.

ALAN: How did Denise take the Jeremy Sandra development?

MYRNA: She was in tears as we were doing the washing up. I tried to reassure her that Tracey was bound to meet somebody else at her age.

ALAN: Do you think she'll have come round now. She was silent at breakfast and seemed pre-occupied.

MYRNA: It was just the initial reaction – I'm sure she'll be okay soon. Mind you – if you hadn't asked the boy's name and then forced me to get in touch with Sandra the unpleasantness wouldn't have happened.

ALAN: That's typical of you – I get the blame for everything. You forget I wasn't all that keen to go in the first place.

MYRNA: Well it wasn't my fault – if you'd have done what you normally do in company – just sitting there like a dumb statue, no one would have been any the wiser. Instead a really lovely day was spoilt.

ALAN: I must admit I do feel a little guilty. I hope everything turns out alright.

(FADE OUT – IT IS ABOUT SIX MONTHS LATER – ALAN HAS JUST RETURNED HOME FROM THE OFFICE)

ALLAN: Hello Gillian – is your mom back yet?

GILLIAN: No she phoned to say she's going straight to Gym from work.

(THE PHONE RINGS)

ALAN: Okay Gillian – I'll take it in the front room. Hello can I help you?

TRACEY: Is that Mr. Dakin.

ALAN: Speaking

TRACEY: This is Tracey Marsden here Denise's daughter. I need some advice.

ALAN: I'll do my best Tracey – by the way how's your mom and dad – getting ready for Christmas I suppose. Hope they are well.

TRACEY: Mom is doing okay – I'm not sure about dad – were no longer on speaking terms.

ALAN: Oh that is sad news. Why what's happened?

TRACEY: The truth is Mr.Dakin I want to become Jewish and would like your guidance on how to go about it.

ALAN: But I thought the relationship with that Jewish young man was over.

TRACEY: It is – it's not because of him I want to convert.

ALAN: Well Tracey I really don't think I'm the best person to speak to about this. Apart from the fact my faith demands that in the first instance

I should put you off. – in your case I'd be helping to destroy your relationship with your father.

TRACEY: But surely as an adult I have a right to make my own decisions and my father should recognise it – my mom does.

ALAN: That may well be so Tracey – but as a friend of your parents it wouldn't seem right. Tell you what phone me same time tomorrow.

TRACEY: Very well I'll do that.

ALAN: Gillian – don't put my dinner out yet – I've got to make a phone call hello – Denise this is Alan Dakin speaking – I've just had a call from Tracey and —

DENISE: Actually sir our business does not handle that sort of work now.

ALAN: Do I take it there is no communication between you and Tracey now?

DENISE: That's right

ALAN: And does that mean Myrna and I are no longer regarded as your friends?

DENISE: Well as I say sir – that sort of business is no longer done by our

Company. We do find it embarrassing having to turn away so many good customers.

ALAN: I hope Charlotte is well and I regret the situation – goodbye .

(LATER THAT EVENING)

MYRNA: Don't be too upset – and don't say anything to Tracey if she phones back. I'll talk to Denise I've got her private number at work. I'll get in touch tomorrow and let you know the outcome tomorrow night.

(THE FOLLOWING EVENING)

ALAN: Did you manage to phone Denise?

MYRNA: Yes – it's a sad situation. It seems that Tracey became interested in Judaism long before she met Jeremy Khanmann.

ALAN: Really – how come?

MYRNA: Just after starting Uni. She showed Tracey the letter you wrote. It so happened that it fitted in with her modern history module. Well anyway shortly afterwards she got involved with you know who. The upshot is Denise and Graham had a row. He blamed her for hanging on to your letter and the family crisis was all her fault.

ALAN: What a terrible mess.

MYRNA: She was in tears as we were speaking. I was also crying because I knew I was losing a good friend. She is so kind and generous and easy to get on with. You've no idea what its like having somebody sensible and friendly to talk to – instead of those moaning dreary yentas in the charity groups.

ALAN: What should I say to Tracey when she calls back. Maybe you could speak to her instead.

MYRNA: No fear –I'd tell her straight – I don't believe in conversions at all.

(THE PHONE RINGS)

ALAN: Oh heck! I'll bet that's Tracey. Well here goes. Hello is that Tracey. Right well okay. All I can say is I can't stop you looking in the Telephone directory and looking up Synagogue. They're the best people to give advice. I just hope and pray Tracey that you will make your peace with your father. Anyway whatever the outcome I wish you the best of luck. Bye

(THREE YEARS LATER)

MYRNA: Here – just look at this. The Ladies Synagogue cultural group have sent this circular.

ALAN: Let's have a gander. The Ladies Blah! Blah! Blah! Didee Blah! At six p.m. Thursday the —

MYRNA: See what I mean? What a daft time. Working women will have just finished work. The housewives will be preparing meals for Shabbat. They are about as incompetent as the dozy men I work with. And just who is going to be interested in that subject after just finishing work?

ALAN: Oh yes the subject. Mysticism, Kabala and the Jewish Woman. Guest speaker Rebbitzen Ruth Simchoni of Jerusalem. I've heard of her husband Rabbi simchoni – He's a well known Kabalist. What does it say about her? I'll just read her c.v. It says Rebbitzen Simchoni is in great demand as a speaker in Israel by religious women's groups. She is regarded as the expert on issues affecting Jewish religious women. She was born in . . .   Bloody hell fire I don't

MYRNA: Language Alan – What's the matter?

ALAN: What' the matter – What's the matter? Just read the c.v. from the second paragraph.

MYRNA: Give it here – I don't what you are getting hett up about.

ALAN: Just read it – go on read.

MYRNA: Okay! Okay! Calm down. She was born in Kirklevington a small village in north east England to a Church of England it can't be! But it!

ALAN: It most certainly is and what's more if I'd been allowed to make a phone call all those years ago instead of writing a letter – this would never have happened.

THE END